BEHIND THE WALLS

A DCI PILGRIM CRIME THRILLER
BOOK 4

By
A L Fraine

Book List

www.alfraineauthor.co.uk/books

Acknowledgements

Thank you to my wife Louise for her tireless support, my kids for being amazing, and my family for believing in me.

Thank you to my amazing editor Crystal Wren for her critical eye and suggestions, they're always on point.

Thank you to my fellow authors for their continued inspiration.

And finally, thank you to you, the readers, for reading my crazy stories.

Table of Contents

1

Bringing her trusty little hatchback to a stop on the residential street, Helen pulled the handbrake on. Closing her eyes, she killed the engine and took a long breath as she prepared herself for another meeting with her brother.

Another meeting that would likely prove to be just as fruitless as the last one, but she had to try.

He was her brother, and frankly, he deserved better than this.

She hated what her father had done to him, how he treated his one and only son. She hated that Mark felt he couldn't live at home anymore, that he felt ostracised by the very people who should love him the most.

But maybe she could turn that around. Maybe she was his one lifeline, his one chance of having a family. She wasn't about to abandon him, even if he ended up hating her for it.

She just wanted what was the best for him and the family, and she would do what was necessary to make that happen.

Taking another long breath, she regarded the terrace house across the street, with its tired façade and dark windows. The street was not a wealthy one, with its packed-in, cramped housing, messy three-metre deep front gardens and banged up cars parked haphazardly. There was probably a drug problem here, too, if she had to guess. It was that kind of place.

Thinking of Mark living here made her feel sick to her stomach. But what could she do?

Well, she'd do whatever was needed to put things right. She had to because no one else would.

Steeling herself for the confrontation to come, she climbed out of her car and crossed the street.

Approaching the house, she noted the single parked-up van outside the property before turning in and walking up to the front door. All the windows were dark. It didn't look like he was here, so maybe this was a fruitless endeavour anyway.

Had he moved on already? He'd only been here a few weeks. She wondered how that would go down with the landlord. Not well, she guessed... if she was right.

If he had moved on, she hoped he'd paid this one and not stiffed her too. He'd end up blacklisted for good if he wasn't careful. Shaking her head, she reached for the door and noticed it swing in slightly as she rapped her knuckles against the wood. The sight of the open door gave her pause as she wondered why on earth he'd leave the front door open on a street like this?

Unless someone had broken in... or he was in trouble of some kind?

Suddenly concerned for Mark's welfare, she pushed the door wide and stepped inside.

"Mark?"

No answer. The house was dark and quiet. She had a feeling that no one had been here for a while, but it was strange because it also felt like she wasn't alone.

Someone was in here. She felt sure of it.

"Mark? Are you here?"

Again, there was nothing, just silence. She glanced right into the front room, but there was no one there. Just well-used furniture on worn carpet that badly needed replacing.

Turning, she assessed the corridor before approaching the stairs and looking up. Was he in here? Had he fallen somewhere and needed her help? Or...

She had visions of finding him dead, sitting in a seat or lying in bed. Maybe he'd overdosed? She knew he used occasionally and hoped it wasn't that. The thought alone sent a shiver down her spine.

No, it couldn't be that. It couldn't *possibly* be that. She needed to remain positive and think good thoughts. She'd find him asleep, maybe.

With a frown, she turned back to the front door, the one she'd just closed. But if he was sleeping, why would he have left the door open?

He was probably drunk. Drowning his sorrows, most likely. He could have forgotten to close the door when he stumbled back. Yeah, that felt like it fit better in her mind.

Looking back up the stairs, she placed a foot on the first step and heard a sudden thud. But it didn't come from upstairs. It came from down here, further in. Did it come from below her?

Did this place have a basement?

Helen walked around and along the hall, finding that the door under the stairs was ajar. She pulled it wide and saw a glow of light down below.

So he was here, she concluded with a smile, swiftly followed by a frown as she pondered why he'd be in the basement.

"Mark, are you down there?"

There was no answer.

Helen found herself rooted to the spot, torn between walking down the old stairs or running from the house.

But why? Why did this scare her so much?

She knew her brother was here just a few days ago. He was renting it, so it must be him down there for some god-awful reason. She just found herself at a loss as to why.

But, if he'd been drinking again and fallen, maybe... maybe he needed her help. He could be dying down there, and she was just a few metres away, scared of a basement.

She shook her head in a vain attempt to banish the silly fears that had blossomed in her mind for no good reason, and think rationally about this. This wasn't some stupid horror film where the ditzy blonde investigated a dark barn only to find some monstrous creature from a nightmare waiting in the darkness for her.

This was real life, and she wasn't blonde. Instead, what she did know was that her brother needed help.

Mark was not in a good place mentally, with everything that had been going on, and he was renting this dingy place because of her stupid ass dad. She was his one chance of getting out of here, or at least, that's what she thought, anyway. That's what she hoped.

She knew he didn't *quite* see it that way, that he didn't appreciate her sticking her nose into his life, but she couldn't just leave him. He was her brother. She had to help.

It was a sister's duty to stand side by side with her family and do whatever was needed to help them.

With that thought foremost in her mind, she set off down the stairs, making for the single light source, mentally preparing herself for what she might find.

At the bottom of the stairs, she turned left and looked across a mostly empty space. There were some racks along one wall. Stones and loose debris littered the concrete floor.

She noted some cardboard boxes that had seen better days, rags, and little else. Certainly no sign of Mark.

Weird.

She felt sure she'd heard something, some kind of movement. Maybe she'd been mistaken? Maybe it was next door?

The single bare bulb burnt bright, hanging from a cord on the ceiling with a dangling pull chain.

Maybe he was upstairs, and she was mistaken in thinking someone was down here. Helen walked over and pulled the cord. For a moment, the world went pitch black. Blinking as her eyes adjusted to the darkness, she was soon able to pick out the stairs and the door at the top where dim light leaked into the basement.

She made for it, feeling unsteady on her feet in the darkness.

Movement. She heard something shift and looked round to see another light source as if it were... but no, that was impossible.

What the hell?

That hadn't been there a moment ago.

A shadow moved across the light. Someone was in here with her.

"Urgh," she yelped before someone grabbed her and dragged her kicking and screaming away from the stairs and freedom.

2

"Here you go, Mr Pilgrim," the woman said as she handed over the keys to the house with a smile on her face. "You're officially the new owner."

Jon took the keys and smiled at her. "Thank you."

"That's it now," Kate remarked from his left. "You're stuck here. You're officially a southerner. Welcome to the family."

Jon gave her a look with one raised eyebrow. "Hardly."

"You're going to have to start talking like us, sooner or later."

"Says the Irish girl! To be sure, to be sure. Potatoes!" he replied, putting on an admittedly terrible Irish accent.

Kate raised a middle finger. "We'll get to you eventually. Then it'll be 'barth', not 'bath' and 'grarss' not 'grass'. You know it's only a matter of time, Jon. Why fight it?"

"I shall put up a valiant resistance to the southern taint, on behalf of my northern heritage."

"Oh no," Kate said as she haunched over. She hissed her words and wrung her hands through one another. "It's only a matter of time. Soon, you will be one of us."

"You can be really quite scary when you want to be. You know that?"

"One of us, one of us, one of us…" she muttered and giggled.

"And yet, I find it slightly arousing," he said, suggestively.

"And on that note, I'll be off," the Agent said. "I hope you get settled in soon."

Kate watched the agent walk off with a smile and a wave. "You scared her off."

"That's rich, coming from the Tea Witch."

"My tea's always rich and flavoursome, I'll have you know. Few can withstand its charms."

Jon stared at her for a moment. "You're really going all-in with this witch thing, aren't you?"

"Just rolling with the punches, dear. Now come on, let's get these boxes inside. Try your keys out."

Jon turned to face the Guildford townhouse that was now his. The tall, three-storey, dark brick building was his. No more hotel rooms or sleeping on Rachel's sofa. He had a home. A place of his own, and it felt good. It was a big step, for sure, and it was the first place he'd owned since the house in Nottingham, the one he'd bought with Charlotte.

But now, here he was, over a hundred miles away, moving into a new home without her.

Part of him felt sad that his life had moved on so completely from what it had been before, but he knew that had been inevitable. He couldn't stay in that house, in

13

Nottingham, moping about his dead girlfriend forever. There was so much more to life than that. And it was only a small, nagging part of him that felt that way. For the most part, he was happy. Thrilled even, that he had found his way again after being lost for so long, and part of that was because of the young woman who stood beside him, eager to get into the house and help him move in.

And so here he was, several months into his new job on the SIU, with a new home and a girlfriend he found he loved as much as he had Charlotte.

Life wasn't that bad really, not anymore.

He missed Charlotte. He felt he probably always would. Those thoughts of 'what if' would never go away. But he couldn't, and wouldn't, dwell on them. That way lay madness and loneliness, and he would not go there.

Stepping up to the house, he pushed the key into the lock. He jiggled it around a bit before looking back at Kate, putting a worried expression on his face.

"Oh…" he said, rattling the key again. "Oh no."

"What?"

"I can't… it won't…"

"You're kidding! But, she's gone," Kate replied, looking along the road to where the agent had driven off.

With her gaze averted, Jon unlocked the door and opened it, waiting for her to look around.

"You could jump in your car quickly. I'm sure you could catch her up…" she said, before looking back.

Jon looked quite amused as he held the door open.

Kate gave him a look, sticking out her bottom lip. "Git."

"I know, but I'm your git. Come on, let's have look inside."

"I wonder what I see in you sometimes, you know?" she grumbled as she followed him in.

The house was basically identical to how it had looked on his previous visits. He spotted a few more cobwebs than before up in the corners, but they would be easily dealt with. Jon stood in the hall and smiled as he took a breath, satisfied. This would be a good home, he thought. A new start, and a place to make new memories. His old life up in Nottingham seemed like it had all happened so long ago now, as if it had happened to someone else, and he realised that a clean break had been just what he had needed. Others had told him this back up north, including Damon, but he'd resisted. He'd felt like he would be betraying Charlotte by moving away and starting afresh.

But now he knew he'd been wrong in that assessment, and he also knew that Charlotte would never have wanted him to mope about the rest of his days, lamenting what could have been. She might have been his partner and had loved him dearly, but she'd also been quite a practical woman in certain regards and would want him to live a rich and fulfilling life.

As these thoughts raced through his mind, while his eyes scanned over the hallway and the rooms, he started to feel a little emotional, but in a good way.

"Are you alright?" Kate asked, a hint of concern in her voice.

"Yeah. I'm fine," he replied, with a sniff, blinking back the tears that were threatening to well up.

"It's a big step, I guess," Kate said, looking up at him. She probably realised what he was thinking about.

"Yeah. It is. But a good one." Kate was well aware of his past and the shadow of Charlotte that hung over him sometimes.

"Come on, we've got a load of stuff to move in. Let's get on with it."

Jon nodded, knowing she was trying to distract him and stop him from becoming melancholy, but it was the right thing for her to do, and he appreciated her attempts to keep him on track.

He followed her back out to the rented van he'd been using to ferry his stuff from the storage place. He'd probably need to make a couple more trips. Plus, there were all the white goods to get delivered and installed too. He was going to be busy working on the house for weeks. Actually, it was probably going to be months, given the nature of his work.

Setting himself to the task, he started lifting boxes and furniture from the van and into the house. Trying to make sure he put the right bits in the right rooms to minimise work later.

They ended up taking another trip to the lockup to pick up more stuff and set to transferring that load into the house as well. It was back-breaking work, but there was an element of fun to it, as he figured out which room was which and where things were going to live.

He'd never been a fan of moving house. The whole thing was just so much bother and hassle when all Jon wanted from his life outside of work was peace and quiet. His and Kate's work lives were so full of drama and chaos that he wanted to keep that at arm's length as much as possible.

Of course, that wasn't always possible, but he did his best.

"Cup of tea?" Kate asked, holding the kettle aloft, having plucked it from a box.

"Yeah," he replied with a sigh. "Aaah, oi. Hold up. This is my house, and I want to make the first cuppa, and it'll be a proper brew, made the way it should be made, too."

"And how's that? With gravy and Whippet piss?"

"Aye, something like that, lass," he said, walking over and taking the kettle from her hand. "Watch and learn, Barry, watch and learn."

"Oh, I am. Dating you has been a constant education, believe me."

"It's good to learn about different ways of life, though, right?"

"I guess. At least I know how not to live mine."

"And yet you bought into it by agreeing to date me."

"What can I say? I could see you needed a guiding hand, someone to look after you and show you what you were missing out on."

"What, like humous, and quinoa?"

"Something like that."

"What about these?" Jon asked, pulling a packet of Fig Rolls from the shopping bag he'd brought in with him.

Kate gasped. "Oh, well, now you're talking. If you keep feeding me those, I'll be here all night."

"You really are a sucker for them, aren't you?"

"They're like mana from heaven. You like them, right?"

"I do, actually," Jon admitted. "Unlike Nathan."

"See, my positive influence is rubbing off on you. Now, gimmie!" She snatched the packet from him as Jon returned to making tea. Kate pulled out a Fig Roll and took a bite as if it was the most amazing thing she'd ever tasted.

"Careful, I might think you enjoy that more than you like me."

"I'll admit, it's a close call."

"I think I have a few advantages over a Fig Roll."

"One or two, but let's not get carried away."

"I did buy them."

"I know, and I shall be forever grateful to you for it."

"Forever?"

"Well, maybe for the next few hours," she replied with a shrug before she stepped up to him and pulled him in for a hug and a brief kiss.

"Oooh, figgy," Jon replied, licking his lips before pouring the tea and making a point of adding the milk second, after the water.

"I suppose if I'm going to be dating you, I need to get used to that."

"We all make sacrifices, my dear." He winked and handed her a mug.

"Thank you, and yes, I guess we do. You must be happy with this house then? It's lovely, really. There's a lot of potential."

"Yeah, I am. I think I'll be happy here."

"I hope so."

"Oh? Thinking of hanging around, are you?"

"I might, you know… if you're lucky," she replied. "I'll need to train you up, of course, but I'm up to that challenge."

"Yeah, good luck with that," Jon replied, scoffing at her comment.

She laughed. He enjoyed listening to her and the banter they had between them. She gave as good as she got, and he liked that about her.

They were soon back to work, unloading and unpacking, as Jon started to settle into the house, finding new homes for his stuff.

He found a few photos of Charlotte he'd packed into one of the storage boxes, and it brought him up short for a moment. He picked one of them up and gazed at her smiling face as she beamed out at him. She'd been beautiful, but she was also long gone, and there was no bringing her back.

He'd kept these photos up in his old house, doing his best to keep her fresh in his memory. It was as if he'd been trying to keep her alive. He didn't want to forget her, or what she'd looked like, but he guessed he'd never really forget. Not really.

Placing the framed photo back in the box with the others, he heard Kate moving about downstairs. She wouldn't mind if he had a photo or two of her out, but he realised he didn't want to have all of them up. It would seem odd, and would be too much of a reminder about what happened to her.

One or two would be okay, he thought, but that's all. There was no need for any more.

Standing up, Jon walked to the front window. He was in one of the upstairs rooms at the front of the house, which he thought he might use as a spare room for guests. For now, it would be a suitable dumping ground for some of the boxes when he wasn't sure where something might go.

Jon looked out onto the street, noting Kate bringing in another box from the van.

Across the street, he noticed a single man standing against a hedge, looking at his house.

He wore a hooded coat, and he couldn't quite make out the details in his face in the evening light. But as he watched, the man very clearly looked up and locked eyes with him.

The man stood there for a moment longer, staring at him, before he slowly tore his eyes away and walked away up the street.

Jon watched him go, wondering who he was and why he was staring at the house. Maybe he was the local weirdo or an overly enthusiastic member of the neighbourhood watch group. Jon couldn't be sure but made a note to keep an eye out for him.

Shaking his head, Jon returned to unpacking.

3

"Thanks for all your help last night," Jon said as he walked with Kate towards the front door. "I couldn't have done as much without you."

"That's okay, happy to help. Also, I know what you keep in your drawers now, so..." She bugged her eyes at him.

Jon raised an eyebrow and smiled. "Hopefully, I didn't scare you off."

"Nah. I'm made of tough stuff, and I'll turn you into a southerner yet."

"Don't start that again. I'll always be northern, no matter how long I'm down here. But, I'll admit, I have a soft spot for a few of you southerners," he replied with a wink.

Kate placed a hand on her chest. "Oh, be still my beating heart. I'm so flattered."

"Seriously though, thank you for helping and staying over. I know you hadn't planned to."

She shrugged. "I know, but I just didn't fancy going home, so..."

"I suppose it meant we got to christen the place," he said with a wink, wondering if that was a bit of a crass thing to say.

"Eeeww, Jon! You make it sound like a dog marking his territory."

Jon blinked. "Aaah, well, that's certainly an image I'm not getting out of my head anytime soon. Thanks for that."

"You started it, you big lug." She pulled him in for a hug and a quick kiss. "I'll see you later."

"Sure thing," he said, moving toward the door. "What time do you think you'll be over?"

"Early afternoon? I've just got a few errands to run and shopping to get. I've got nothing in my flat. All the usual stuff when we have a couple of days away from the station, you know? But I'll be back to help you later. Don't worry. I know you can't cope without me."

"Oh, indeed. I'd just fall to bits without you here."

"I know, it's very sad. Try to cope without me, won't you."

"I'll try. Besides, I'll just lure you back with more Fig Rolls."

"Damn it, my one weakness!" she said, opening the door. She kissed him again and walked out. He had a few things to do today too, but most of his time would be spent here, moving things, unpacking things, taking deliveries. He wondered if he'd ever feel settled.

But that was the thing with homes, wasn't it? They were a constant money pit, and they always needed things doing to them. It was never-ending.

Looking at the ceiling, he wondered what secrets this home would hold. All homes had them buried away. He'd paid for a survey, of course, but they never revealed every little problem a house had.

But, he was sure things would become apparent and be revealed in due course. He just hoped they wouldn't be too bad.

He walked back towards the kitchen with a sigh, where he'd left the dregs of his morning tea, which he'd finish before getting on with the day's tasks. He wanted to get as much done as he could before returning to work tomorrow. He had his own run to the shops to do for a start. He couldn't live on takeaways, not if he wanted to keep running after criminals.

He'd barely stepped back into the kitchen when there was a sudden knock on the door.

Jon smirked as his eyes picked out the half-eaten packet of Fig Rolls on the side and wondered if she'd decided to grab one last one before she set off.

"Alright, alright. You can have one for the road," he called out as he walked back up the corridor and pulled the door open.

"Well, that's a hell of an offer, Jon," Sydney said.

The raven-haired woman leant against the door frame and beamed at him with her glistening ruby lips. Her dusky eyes bored deep into his soul, promising him all kinds of things. She was all hips and boobs in her body-hugging dress, and she clearly knew the effect it would have.

For a moment, Jon wasn't sure how to react. He'd not seen Sydney since the end of the Russell Hodges case. She'd sent him a few messages in the interim, but he'd never replied as he did not want to encourage her. But, it *seemed* she didn't *need* any encouragement.

She'd shown some kind of interest in him during that earlier case, flirting with him mercilessly, despite being Russell's supposed girlfriend, although she was no longer with him now, as far as he knew.

He couldn't quite believe she was here, on his doorstep right now, especially so soon after Kate had left. What if she'd appeared while Kate was still here? What would Kate have said?

But no, if he had to guess, she'd probably been watching the house and had waited until Kate walked away before making her move. She was that kind of person.

Cunning, smart, sexy and dangerous. Especially that last one. Kate had seen it too. She was trouble in high heels.

So, what was she doing here? Why had she suddenly appeared on his doorstep? He dreaded to think, and in fact, he really didn't want to know. He just wanted to get rid of her.

But before he could get his thoughts together enough to slam the door in her face, she barged past him. Walking into his new home, her shiny black stilettos clicked on his wooden flooring. She walked in them like they were a natural extension of her feet, confident and assured, despite them looking like some kind of torture devices.

He watched her swan down his hallway, her hips swinging as she traced a finger along the wall, no doubt entirely aware that his eyes were on her. But he wasn't looking at her in that way. He had no interest in her beyond her connection to the case she'd been a part of. Instead, he just felt horrified that she was here at all.

"So, this is your new place, is it, Jon? Hmm… Well, I guess you could say this is… well, *nice*, I guess?"

With a grimace from her backhanded compliment, Jon leaned out through the door. Looking up the street to where he knew Kate's car had been parked, he noted it was gone, and he breathed a sigh of relief. He wasn't quite sure how Kate would react to Sydney appearing on his doorstep.

Pleased that this visit hadn't caused any further issues, he turned and steeled himself for the conversation to come.

"What are you doing here, Sydney?" he asked, holding the door open for a moment.

"Sydney?" She looked back, a carefully sculpted eyebrow raised. "Oh yes, I guess that was the name you knew me by.

Hmm, no. I think we need to change that. My name is not Sydney."

"You've mentioned that before. But that's the name I know you by, so..."

"Then get used to something else, Jon."

Jon grunted in exasperation.

"Hmm. You can call me, Ariadne."

"Ariadne?"

"Do you like it?"

"Only as much as I like you, which is to say, not at all."

"Oh, come now, Jon, don't be mean. Is that any way to treat a guest who's come here in good faith to congratulate you on your new home, such as it is? Please, have some manners."

"That's rich, coming from you."

"Trying to ruffle my feathers, Jon?" She smiled at him, and then turned away, keeping her eyes on him before looking away at the last moment, as she set off down the hallway. "Shut the door, Jon. I'm not leaving yet, not without a guided tour."

Jon grumbled under his breath. For a moment, he considered grabbing and carrying her outside just to get rid of her. But knowing Sydney, or Ariadne, or whatever, she'd find a way to make his life difficult, and it wouldn't do for him to get accused of that kind of thing, no matter who said it.

He guessed he'd just have to see where this went, he thought, and closed the door with a long sigh. Walking after her, he pointed to the floor.

"Hallway," he said, and pointed to the room on his right. "Dining room." Jon continued to point at things and state loudly what they were as he walked back towards the kitchen at the back of the house. "Living room, boxes, stairs, walls, kitchen. It's nothing you've not seen before."

"Oh Jon, you really are a sourpuss. Here I am, being nice to you, and all you can do is be sarcastic and rude?"

"I'm a northerner. It's a way of life," he replied, falling back on a typical stereotype.

"Hmm." She muttered, leaning over the sink to look through the back window into the overgrown garden beyond. It might be his imagination, but he got the feeling she bent forward just a little more than she really needed as if she was displaying her rear for him. She was flirting. But why? What did she want from him?

Following her gaze out the window, he saw the overgrown grass just looked like a lot of work, so he turned away. He'd deal with that later.

"Nice garden," Ariadne remarked as she stood up straight again and tilted her head to catch his eye. "Lot's of space to, well, do all kinds of things."

Her words just sounded dirty. They dripped with innuendo, which was no doubt on purpose.

"Why did you come here, Syd... Ariadne?"

"See, you're getting it." She sauntered over to a nearby chair.

"Am I? Well, I'll tell you one thing I don't get, your interest in me."

Ariadne sat and took her time crossing her legs as she settled into the seat. "Well, what can I say? You just intrigue me, Jon. I like you, and I feel bad that you lost out on coming with me. I really am quite rich now, you know."

At the cost of someone else, he thought. "How is, Russell Hodges?" he asked pointedly.

"Why should I care?"

"You fleeced him. You stole from him."

"Any man who can't look after and hold on to his own money doesn't deserve to have it."

"You're lucky he didn't press charges."

"Luck's got nothing to do with it, Jon. You should know that. Only an idiot relies on luck. Besides, he wouldn't do that to me, and even if he did, who would he prosecute? Sydney? She doesn't exist."

"You exist," Jon replied.

"Prove it. You know, you really should see where I live now, Jon. It's quite spectacular, and it could have been yours too."

"I'm quite happy here, thanks."

"You should never settle for second best, you know. If you want something, you should get out there and take it."

"Is that your philosophy on life?"

She stood, her eyes locked on his. "Oh yes. I always have my eyes on the next thing I want, and I always get it," she answered, walking over to him, her movements languid and calculated.

"Always?" Jon asked, feeling very uncomfortable.

"Always," she replied, getting closer. She reached out and placed a finger on his chest.

Jon stepped sideways and slipped away from her. "I think it's time for you to leave, Ariadne."

"You got it right. Well done." She sighed dramatically. "Okay, I'll go. But I'll see you again soon, Jon."

"I can't wait," he replied, making sure to put as much sarcasm into the words as he could, before walking up the hallway with her right behind him, her shoes ringing out on the hard flooring.

"It's a nice place you have here, Jon. Cute, and small, but nice. I'm sure you'll be happy here."

"I will be in a minute," Jon remarked, lacing his words with meaning.

She smiled, her crimson lips flashing. "I'll see you soon."

"Bye," Jon said. He closed the door on her before locking the deadbolt and walking away. He could still smell her perfume and shook his head as he walked into the front room. Peering out the front window of what would be his lounge, he watched her walk out to the pavement. She paused and looked back, her eyes falling on the front window he was behind. She blew him a kiss and waved, before turning and walking along the road to where a black Lamborghini Centenario with red detailing sat waiting. It had already drawn a small crowd of admirers. She seemed to relish their attention as she climbed in, revved the engine, and screeched off down the road, much to the delight of the watching kids.

But Jon felt none of that exhilaration. He felt only troubled and concerned. What was her game? Why was she interested in him? There were no good answers to these questions, and that was a concern.

4

Lenny stood in the playroom at the back of the house, looking at the wall that adjoined the kitchen, and considered what his first move should be.

The wall, like half of them in this quirky little cottage, was unusually thick and uneven, betraying the building's age. They'd fallen in love from the moment they'd seen it and knew they had to own it. It was just so quaint and oldy-worldy, he thought. But that wouldn't stop him from doing some work on it. There were a number of things he wanted to do to make it theirs, not least of which was to fix some of the dodgy wiring and sort out the central heating. The place just got so cold, despite the thick walls.

And then there was the wifi, which had trouble reaching all corners of the house, again because of the walls. He'd ended up buying several extenders just to fix it.

But his next project was a little more involved and would leave them in something of a mess for a while. But, it would be worth it.

The whole house was a series of small rooms, and to Lenny, it desperately needed opening up. Luckily, Phoebe agreed.

Areas like between the kitchen and this back room, which had ended up as Gracie's playroom, were ripe for adjusting. Knocking through would open the whole thing up and create a nice large space for them, which would be ideal.

"Have you broke the wall yet, Daddy?" Gracie asked, wandering through, clutching her favourite doll.

"Not yet, sweety, no. It's going to take a while to do," he replied and crouched down before her.

"Oh, But I want to play in here."

"You can't today, remember. You need to play in the lounge, okay? Daddy's going to make a lot of mess."

"Oh. Okay."

He smiled at her as she turned and walked out, pausing to wave at him in the doorway before she disappeared. Once she was gone, he returned his attention to the wall, feeling both keen to get on but also slightly nervous about taking his sledgehammer to it.

He'd done his homework, though, and knew it wasn't a load-bearing wall, so there really wasn't much that could go seriously wrong. Lenny took a deep breath and picked up the hammer, only for the doorbell to sound through the house.

"Can you get that, please, Lenny?" Phoebe called out from another room.

"Yeah, I'll go," Lenny replied as he strode through the house, leaving the hammer behind. "It'll be the builder's merchants, anyway."

Opening the door, he was greeted by a stout, overweight man in a high-vis vest over a check shirt and jeans.

"Mr Woods?" the man asked.

"That's me," Lenny replied. "Hi."

"Hello. I've got bricks, sand and cement for you. Am I okay to just put it on the driveway?"

"Yeah, sure."

"Right you are then," the man answered, and wandered back to his truck.

"Where's he putting it?" Phoebe asked, joining him at the door a few moments later.

"Just on the driveway."

"What did I say, Leonard? It'll look ugly there. Can't we move it to the side or back?"

Lenny sighed. "That's a bit difficult to do."

"It'll be better for you if it's closer to the back of the house and won't be an eyesore. Ask him what he can do, please."

Lenny nodded, knowing better than to look too annoyed. "Sure thing, I'll ask."

"Thank you," Phoebe declared, apparently satisfied. "And if he can't do that, maybe you can move it later?"

He watched her walk away, after a brief smile, and knew that if the driver just dumped them on the driveway, he'd end up having to move them himself, brick by brick.

The embarrassment of asking was worth it, just to try and avoid having to move the things himself. Stepping out of the house, he walked towards the truck, where the driver was already moving the lifting arm into position.

He sighed as he walked, annoyed that Phoebe would be so annoyed by some bricks, but he guessed if it made her happy, then it was worth it.

"Hey, um, how far around the house can you put the bricks?" he asked as he approached the driver.

The man turned and gave him a look. "Around the house?"

"Yeah, sorry. Just, you know, the wife isn't keen on them being out front."

The man gave him a look that was somewhere between pity and understanding as he sighed and stopped moving the lifting arm. "I can't get them to the back, but I can maybe slot them down the side there. Will that do?"

"You're a lifesaver," Lenny replied with a smile.

The man grunted. "Yeah, I know." Lenny watched as he climbed back into the cab. As the truck started to move, he noticed a man standing at the end of his driveway, watching.

Lenny recognised him right away, and his stomach tied itself into a knot in anticipation.

"What are you doing?" the man asked.

"Hi Evan," Lenny replied. "Nothing much, just a little home improvement."

"Why?"

He sounded offended. Lenny paused as his chest tightened. He felt sure he knew where this conversation was going, which was essentially nowhere. He was aware of Evan's link to the house, and honestly, he did feel bad for him, but that was a long time ago, and he really did need to move on. This was their home now.

"Because the house is in desperate need of it." Lenny attempted to keep his exasperation at bay.

"No, it's not. It's fine as it is. You need to learn to respect the history of things, Mr Woods, before you go trampling all over it. Have you got planning permission to do whatever it is you're doing?"

"I don't need planning permission, Evan. I know what I'm doing. I am an architect, after all."

Evan looked pissed off as he ground his teeth together. "Well, I don't like it."

"Excuse me for being blunt, Evan, but it's not your house."

"It was, once."

"But not anymore."

36

Evan gave Lenny a frown and screwed up his mouth before he turned and stormed off up the street and back to his house. Lenny watched him go before returning his attention to the driver and the placement of the bricks. They managed to get them quite far back. In the end, and Lenny felt confident that Phoebe would be happy when the driver eventually left.

"Are they at the side?" Phoebe inquired as he stepped back into the house.

"They are," he confirmed.

"See, I knew it wouldn't be an issue. Thank you, sweety."

Lenny gave himself a thin smile as he walked back into the playroom and the wall that he needed to demolish.

Well, there was nothing for it now. He needed to make a start, he thought, and picked up the sledgehammer again. After a moment of consideration, he swung the tool and started to knock out the bricks, such as they were in this old building.

The first one was perhaps the hardest of the lot, and it took him a while to break through the plaster and get the right angle on the uneven brick. But he persisted, and before long, had the first one out. Pleased with his work, he started on the next one.

The bricks after that first one were easier, and he was soon making good progress, but he was surprised just how thick the wall was. It was crazy, but seemed very much in keeping with the rest of the house.

To his knowledge, it was one of the oldest houses in the village and had been here for a long time.

Pressing on, he knocked out a few more, and then noticed something odd. The next brick he found was a modern one.

"Huh," he muttered to himself as he took a closer look. There was a cavity in the wall behind it too.

Lenny didn't spend too long thinking about the oddities of the house, though. He'd never get anything done if he did that. This place was seemingly made of quirks and strangeness. But that was also its charm and what had attracted them to it in the first place.

Pressing on, Lenny started knocking out the modern bricks, which came out so much easier than the irregular shaped old ones, revealing more of the cavity. There wasn't any insulation at all, but he could see something in there; something wrapped in black plastic, like a bin bag. As he knocked out another brick, something shifted, and the plastic fell to the side so that it stuck out.

Lenny stared at the plastic-covered shape. He couldn't really say why, or what caused it, but he got a sudden, sinking feeling, like a huge emptiness that opened up deep inside him and gripped him like a vice.

Something was wrong here, very badly wrong. And yet, he found himself wanting to know what it was. What was causing this sudden fear that was clawing at his mind? He had to know and dropped the hammer.

It clunked to the floor as he pulled out the Stanley knife from his pocket and extended the blade. Moving closer, he got a whiff of the rank, musty air that had been trapped in the wall and got right to the back of his throat. He pulled part of the plastic taut and cut it before ripping it open.

It took a moment for him to register what he was seeing and comprehend what it might mean as he stepped back, wanting to keep well away from it now he knew what it was.

He needed to keep Gracie out of here, and he needed to make a phone call.

5

Rising from a fitful, nightmare-filled dream, Helen's first thought was how much everything hurt. Her wrists screamed out in agony as something bit into them, holding them fast. They were squashed behind her and pressed up against a rough, solid surface that was cool to the touch.

As she woke, the pain grew. She tried to pull in a long breath, but her chest hurt. She felt crushed as she sucked in dry, dusty air and opened her eyes to find herself in darkness.

In a moment of panic, she yelled, screamed, struggled and fought, but only succeeded in hurting herself further.

No. Stop, she thought as she hissed against the pain. She pressed her eyes shut again and forced herself to take a long slow breath as she tried to calm herself down. She needed to figure out where she was and what was going on.

She was standing up but could hardly move. Where the hell was she?

The last thing she could remember was something in the darkness of the basement lunging at her. They bore her down and crushed her throat before oblivion had claimed her.

But where the hell was she now? What on earth was this?

She was squashed in between two walls with barely enough space to breathe. The wall was right up against her face and the back of her head. Every movement scratched and scraped against her skin, making movement difficult.

A dim glow from above provided her with a tiny amount of light. She blinked, trying to get her eyes to adjust.

She could feel bindings on her wrists, holding her hands in the small of her back. There were similar constrictions around her knees and ankles too. She'd have fallen over if it wasn't for the wall.

Over the next few moments, her eyes started to get used to the lack of light. She could make out shapes and a few details. Where was the light coming from? Moving slowly, she turned her head and looked up. Above her, a small vent allowed a sliver of light into the space. She could almost feel the fresh air it let in and taste the freedom that it teased. So close, and yet out of reach.

But a vent meant that sound could escape.

Was anyone nearby? Was she still in the same house? Where was she? What had happened to her? She must have been kidnapped and put here. But where was she?

"Help!" she shouted. "Hello? Is there anyone there? Can anyone hear me?"

But she heard nothing in return. No one answered and there were no sounds of movement. Looking right, she saw something shiny, wrapped in black plastic. Blinking to try and make her eyes adjust better, she had the sudden sinking feeling that she knew what was wrapped in the plastic.

"Oh god. No. Oh god, no."

She could make out the distinct shape of a head on a pair of shoulders beneath the plastic, but it wasn't moving at all. Craning her neck, she felt sure she could see more beyond the one closest to her.

With rising terror, she turned her head and looked left. Another human shape, wrapped in plastic.

"Oh, Christ," she muttered, realising she was trapped in here with at least three or four other bodies. "Hello? Is there anyone there? Can someone help me? I'm trapped. Hello? Hello!"

But no matter how hard she called, there was no response. Over time, her calls became shouts and then screams. Panicked, terrified screams until her throat hurt even more than it already did. She started to sob as the reality of the situation took root in her mind.

She was trapped. Hidden away somewhere, and if she had to guess, she felt sure she was sealed up behind a wall or something, and she wasn't alone. Whoever had done this to her had been doing it to others, too.

And then images came back to her, glimpses of the person who'd strangled her into unconsciousness. She had memories of coming to and seeing someone above her before she'd slipped back into her nightmares.

She'd seen who'd done this, she realised.

She'd seen them, clearly. But that didn't help her. If she died here, her memories wouldn't be of any use to anyone.

She couldn't die. Not here, not now. She needed to get out of here. She needed to live. But how?

6

Braking, Jon pulled the car to a stop at the side of the street, in the quiet village of Newdigate. The road was a quiet, rural idyll, with spaced-out homes along a country road. The smattering of police vehicles before him stood in sharp contrast to the village atmosphere. There were already plenty of people standing in small groups, watching proceedings from behind the police tape.

None of this was unusual or surprising to Jon. It was just another day on the force. No, he just felt annoyed that his day off had been brought to a sudden and unceremonious end.

Crime, it seemed, had no respect for his work schedule and would continue regardless of what Jon wanted to do. Still, at least he was in his house now, so perhaps he should be grateful for small mercies. His unpacking, however, would need to wait until later.

He wasn't too sure what this call to attend a crime scene was all about. All he knew was that at least one body had been found, and it looked like there was foul play involved.

Looking across at the quaint cottage at the centre of the cordon, with its whitewashed walls and lush front gardens, it really couldn't look more tranquil and innocent if it tried. But he knew as well as anyone else on this, and any other force, that murder could happen anywhere and often in the most surprising places.

As he sat in the car, checking his phone for any new messages, another car pulled up behind. It was Kate; he recognised the vehicle. And sure enough, he spotted the shock of auburn hair as she climbed out, looking just as frustrated as he felt.

Jon put his phone away and got out as she walked over.

"They really do pick their moments, don't they?"

"You're not kidding," Kate replied. "I've not done half the things I wanted to. I've got no idea when I'll get to go and buy some food. There's nothing in my fridge."

"Mine neither…" Jon mused.

"I think it might help if you had a fridge," she suggested.

"You think?" Jon remarked. "Hmm, good thinking, Batwoman."

"Any idea what this is?"

"Nope, nothing beyond what was in the message. I'm guessing it will be another gruesome scene created by a monster in human skin, that will live with me until the day I die."

"You think?"

"Just a hunch," Jon said.

"The call said a body was found."

"Aye. Come on, let's go and see what fresh hell this will be." He led them towards the cordon, where an officer was engaged in a conversation with a bystander.

"You need to tell me what's going on in there." The man's tone forceful and just a little too confrontational for Jon's liking.

"Sir, please," the officer said. "If you would just like to stand back. We can't give out any details right now."

"But, I need to know. You have to tell me," the bystander demanded. He was a tall man with short hair, and he loomed over the PC.

"Everything okay here?" Jon asked as he walked up, flashing his warrant card.

"Everything's fine, sir," the officer replied.

The bystander caught sight of Jon's ID and looked up at him, and then at Kate.

"You're detectives," he stated.

Restraining himself from making a stinging, sarcastic remark, Jon ignored the man as he stepped under the tape. Kate followed as the officer signed them in.

"Thanks," the officer said.

"No, wait," the bystander said. "You need to tell me what this is all about, detectives. I have a right to know. You have to tell me."

Jon sighed and looked back at the man. He seemed awfully interested in what was going on. Unusually so. "What's your name, sir?"

The man frowned and clamped his mouth shut. "Why do you want to know?"

"You want to know what's happened in here?"

"Yes."

"So do I. I have no idea right now, and no amount of shouting at me is going to get you an answer. But, tell me who you are, and maybe I can help you. Is that a fair exchange?"

The man's eyes flicked back and forth between them before he grunted and turned away in a huff, walking around the cordon and up the street. Jon watched him go, narrowing his eyes at the man as he wondered what that was all about.

"Has he been causing problems?" Jon asked the duty officer.

"No. He's been asking questions, though. He's been here the whole time I have. But, other than being a little... forceful, he's not caused any issues."

"Fair enough," Jon replied. "Let me know if he does."

"Will do."

Jon walked after Kate and moved deeper into the cordon. She raised her eyebrows at him as he caught up. "Have you got a suspect before you've even seen the crime scene?"

"Wouldn't that be wonderful," Jon stated.

"It would make for a nice change of pace."

"Wouldn't it just."

"He's clearly interested in what's going on. Might be worth keeping in mind."

"Sure," he replied and walked to a nearby van, where they were handed some forensics suits.

"I hear congratulations are in order," Sergeant Louis Dyson said as he sauntered over and waited for them to change.

"What?" Jon said. "Barry, you're not pregnant, are you?"

Kate smirked. "Hah! Not likely. Christ!"

"Hell, don't do that to me, Dyson. I nearly had a heart attack."

"Har-di-har," Dyson said. "No, I hear you finally got your own place."

"Oh, right, yeah," Jon said in mock realisation. "I'm officially a Surrey resident, now. I think I need to start talking all posh, like."

"You're enjoying it down here that much, huh?"

"It has its perks," he replied, winking at Kate. "Doubt my bank account will ever recover, though."

"Yeah. I hear you can buy a mansion up north for a penny and the promise of a favour," Dyson said.

"Unlike down here where they want your firstborn child and sexual favours," Jon said. "The price difference is horrendous. I'm surprised anyone can actually live down here."

"It's the next generation I feel sorry for," Kate added. "How kids today will get onto the property ladder, is beyond me. It's ridiculous."

"Well, if they're looking at houses like this one, they might want to think again," Dyson replied, jabbing his thumb at the building behind him.

"That bad, is it?" Jon asked.

"It's messed up, is what it is. I've never seen anything like it, and I've worked on Kate and Nathan's cases."

"Shit," Kate cursed, and gave Jon a look.

"Now, you see, don't do that. You've just gone and given me the willies, you pair of prats."

"So, what's the deal?" Kate asked.

"Best you come in and have a look for yourself. I've kept people going in there to a minimum. Photographer and Examiner have been and gone. Sheridan's in there now with her people."

"Okay, thanks." Jon finished kitting himself out with a mask before walking over to the front door and stepping inside. Following the trail through the property, he glanced into the side rooms as he went. Forensics officers went about

49

their work all through the house, but the main focus was in a backroom, adjoined onto the kitchen.

Walking in, Jon was greeted by several people in protective clothing, picking at the wall between this room and the kitchen. Someone had already smashed a sizable hole in it, and leaning out of it, partially wrapped in black plastic, was a dry, mummified human head.

It looked like it had been dead a while.

"Morning, sir, ma'am," Sheridan said as they walked in. "I heard they called you both in, on your day off. That's poor luck."

"Apparently, we're indispensable," Jon remarked. "I should be pleased, I suppose."

"Well, looks like we have a doozy for you today."

"I can see. A body in a wall?" Jon asked.

"Actually, several," Sheridan replied.

"Bloody hell. How many are we looking at?"

"We think there's at least two more in there, maybe more."

Jon frowned as he looked at the wall. "That's incredibly thick for an interior wall. Isn't that a bit weird?"

"This whole house is weird," Sheridan replied. We think this used to be an outside wall, and the house was added to, but yes, the walls are really thick in several places. A product of its age, we think."

Jon nodded. "Alright, so we have several bodies hidden in the wall. What else can you tell me?"

"I've only been able to look at this one, which had been mummified inside the airtight bag it was in. We'll know more later, but, if I had to guess, I'd say it's been in here for a couple of years, easily. The others, I'm not sure. We'll have to get them out and have a look. If they weren't in an airtight bag or were allowed to rot before being bagged, we might be looking at a few bags of bone soup."

"Bone soup? Is this another southern delicacy I've yet to sample?"

"I don't think you'd want to eat it," Sheridan replied. "It'll be nasty."

"I bet. Apart from them being hidden in a wall, obviously, are there any other signs of foul play you can see yet?"

"Nothing yet that I can see. I'm sure the pathologist will be able to help you with that, though."

"Anything else?"

"Nothing yet, but we need to rip this wall out and see what we can find. We'll run a full sweep around the room first before we start demolishing things, but it's going to get messy in here."

"Of course." He turned on the spot to look at the other walls. "And the other walls?"

"Don't know. Good question. We'll need to check any wall that's wide enough, of course."

"Absolutely. So, what happened? How was this discovered?"

"As far as I know," Sheridan replied. "The owner was knocking through to the kitchen and just happened across it. I think they're at the station. Dyson will know. They're pretty upset by all accounts."

"Okay, great, we'll catch up with them there." As he looked around the room there were several colourful containers containing dolls, legos, games and children's books. "What was this room?"

"The owner said it was the playroom for their daughter."

"Shit." He considered the implications of that. How long had the family been living here? And now knowing that their child had been playing in this room, surrounded by dead people.

The very thought of it was nightmare-inducing, and he wasn't the one that had to live with the knowledge that someone had stored possible murder victims in their house.

It made him think of his own house and wonder what secrets it held. Hopefully nothing as horrific as this.

"I know," Sheridan agreed.

"That's messed up," Kate said.

7

"How's the house move going?" Nathan asked from the door to his office.

"Yeah, okay?" Jon replied as he checked through his notes from the crime scene and what had already been pulled together, making sure he was ready for the interview. "It would be going a hell of a lot better if I wasn't here, of course. But, needs must, I suppose."

"Yeah, criminals gonna criminal," Nathan agreed. "So, we have some bodies in a wall, right?"

"Aye," Jon confirmed. "See what you can dig up."

"Will do," Nathan replied. "Lenny's in interview room one, Phoebe is in room two, and their kid is with a support officer in waiting room two."

"Thanks, man. Appreciate it."

"No worries. You'll be back to unpacking before you know it."

"Oooh, can't wait," Jon said sarcastically as he gathered his notes up and followed Nathan out. Kate was crossing the main office floor to him and nodded as she approached.

"So, who's first?"

"Lenny, I think. He found the bodies."

"I was thinking the same."

"Great minds and all that," Jon remarked. "We'll both talk to the parents, but I think you should talk to the kid alone, without me. What do you think?"

"Sure. We wouldn't want to scare the girl, after all, you big scary man."

"I'm a fluffy teddy bear, really," Jon protested.

"Of course you are," she replied, almost dismissively, their conversation amusing some passers-by on the stairwell.

"I am! I just hide it really well."

"I know you do." Jon wasn't sure she sounded convinced. "So, are you taking the lead with Lenny?"

"Sure," Jon said, as they made their way downstairs.

"Have you seen Stingray yet?"

"Nope." He'd expected to see the Superintendent the moment he got in, but so far, Ray hadn't shown his face, which suited Jon just fine. Of course, he could be testing him, to see if Jon would continue to keep him abreast of the latest developments, so Jon made a mental note to hunt him down before he left the building again. A thought occurred to him. "I'm guessing he's the one who pulled us back in today."

"Then that's on him. I'll be putting the hours in and getting my overtime money's worth from today."

"Good plan," Jon agreed, as they walked into the corridor with the interview rooms along the left wall. The officer on guard acknowledged them before they made their way inside room one, to find Lenny with his duty solicitor, Ana Allen, sitting beside him.

Lenny's eyes scanned him and Kate as they walked in, his face betraying the shock that he was feeling. The events of the morning had apparently shaken him to his core, and Jon had to admit, he would probably harbour similar feelings had he been in the same situation. The very idea that this was a possibility made Jon want to somehow X-Ray the walls of his new house, just to be sure no one had concealed anything suspicious there without his knowledge.

Looking at Lenny with his bloodshot eyes and the drained look of his skin, his gut told him that this wasn't their guy. He hadn't done this. But Jon knew better than to listen to such feelings. They were often wrong, and he needed to be guided by the facts.

Still, he saw no need to charge into this interview like a bull in a china shop. He started as he usually did by introducing himself and Kate, and setting the recorder to start. They went through the usual steps before Jon settled into his seat, ready to see where this interview would take him.

"So, Lenny, tell me about this morning. What happened?"

"I don't know, really. It's all just craziness. I was only doing a bit of home improvement, that's all. I went through all the proper channels, did things as I should, and then this happens and I end up here, being interviewed in a police station."

"So, what did you find? Walk me through it, please."

"I was knocking through into the kitchen, taking the wall down so we can have a more open plan area, you know? I was knocking bricks out with the sledge, and then this thing appeared. It was wrapped in plastic and looked solid and stiff. I was shocked, but I didn't know what it was."

"And you opened it?"

"Yeah. I didn't know what it was, so I had a look. I don't know what I was expecting really but... not that."

"So, what did you do next?"

"I went and told Phoebe and made sure she knew to keep Gracie out of there. Then I called you guys. I didn't know I'd be a suspect."

"Don't worry, Lenny, if you didn't do this, you'll be fine."

"But, I didn't. I couldn't. I have no idea how they got in there. This is as much a shock to me as it is anyone else."

"We understand," Kate replied. "But we need to talk to everyone. This is just routine."

"So, what do you do, Mr Woods?"

"I'm an architect. I work in Guildford."

"And is business good?"

"Very, thank you," he replied with a frown.

"And what does your wife do?" Jon asked.

"Nothing. Housewife, I suppose. Looking after a child is a full-time job."

"Of course," Kate agreed. "And is everything good between you and your wife?"

"Yes, thanks. We're very happy."

"That's good. So, tell me about the house."

"My wife found it. It's lovely, isn't it? Just so quirky."

"And how long have you lived there for?" Jon asked, keen to move it along.

"About a year and a half, I think," Lenny answered. "Not long. We bought it off, um... I think his name was Duncan?"

"Duncan?"

"That's right. He was renting it out, I think. I'm not sure. You'll have to check up on that."

"Don't worry, we will, Mr Woods," Kate replied, taking notes.

"So you had no idea about what was behind that wall?"

"No. Come on. Do you really think I'd smash a hole in the wall and call you guys if I did?"

"Stranger things have happened, Mr Woods," Jon replied. Lenny was right, of course. It made no sense for him to knock the wall out and then call the police. That would be a hell of a bluff to make and would likely backfire spectacularly. Jon felt sure that Lenny was innocent in all this, but they had to make sure that he wasn't involved in some other way.

"So, is there anything else you think we should know?" Kate asked. "Anything strange or significant?"

"Not really, but I suppose there's Evan."

"Who's Evan?"

"A neighbour. He lives up the street and is always sticking his nose in where it's not wanted. I saw him in the crowd when we left the house."

Jon frowned, guessing that Evan was the man at the crime scene, talking to the officer outside. "Tall man, short hair, wearing a green t-shirt?"

"That's him," Lenny confirmed. "He's been causing some problems for a while. He wanted to buy the house at the same time we did, and we ended up in a bidding war for it, but we won. He's been bitter ever since."

"And, he was causing problems today?"

"He saw the delivery of bricks I got and seemed to take offence to me doing some work on the house."

"I see," Jon replied.

"And, that's the only link he has to the house, that he wanted to buy it?" Kate asked.

"No. I think he used to live there when he was younger. I think it was his mother's house. I don't think he liked the idea of me changing it too much."

"Or, he knew what was in the walls?" Jon suggested.

Lenny shrugged. "I don't know. I guess... maybe."

The questions continued for a little while as they went over things again, but there wasn't much else they could get out of Lenny, so they ended the interview and moved on to speak to his wife, Phoebe.

"So, the first time you knew something was wrong was when your husband came to see you?"

"That's right. I went and had a look, but... Oh god. I can't believe we've been living with those bodies hidden in there. Gracie's been playing in there, alone, surrounded by those things." Phoebe swallowed as she held her stomach, turning a distinct shade of green. "Just the thought of it, it's like something from a nightmare. Was it the previous owner? Duncan? He owned it for years, rented it out too. Was it him or one of his tenants? I think you need to find him and ask him these questions, frankly."

"We will," Jon assured her. "We'll follow up on all the leads."

"Good. Now, where is my daughter? When can I see her?"

"Soon," Kate replied, her tone soothing. "We just need to talk to her as well."

"Why? Why do you need to talk to her? She's only five. She wouldn't understand. You'll give her nightmares."

"Don't worry, we'll be very careful. We don't want to scare her, but we need impartial answers without any influence from you."

"This will all be over soon," Jon added. "We'll get you back into the house as soon as we can."

"Do you even want to go back, knowing what was in there?" Kate asked.

It was a valid question, and given what had happened, he doubted many people would want to return to such a house.

"Of course, that house is my dream house. I want this over with, so we can get back to our lives in there. Lenny will agree. He knows I'm right."

Jon believed her. He was starting to see what kind of relationship Lenny and Phoebe had and who was in charge. Phoebe seemed very pleasant and calm most of the time, but she was clearly the dominant party in that relationship.

They soon moved on to Gracie, and Jon watched through a one-way mirror as Kate sat on the carpet with her, playing with the toys in the room and talking to her about the events of the day and her parents. It took a little time, but she soon opened up, responding to Kate's friendly manner and answering her questions without much trouble.

Gracie clearly didn't know anything about the bodies in the walls, but she did provide a nice little insight into her parent's relationship, confirming Jon's thoughts that Gracie's mother was very much in charge.

Seeing Kate's way with the girl was lovely to see too. She had a way with children that Jon envied and came to the conclusion that she would make a great mother one day.

With that final interview out of the way, Gracie was reunited with her parents. They left the station, heading for Gracie's grandparents where they would be staying until things calmed down.

"What do you think?" Kate asked as they sat in the waiting room Gracie had been in.

"My gut says they had nothing to do with it. I think they were just a victim of circumstance, rather than a part of anything sinister. But, I've been wrong before. I'm not ready to rule them out yet."

"Then you and I are in agreement. They didn't do this."

"As far as we know," Jon added.

"Yeah, as far as we know. So, what's next?"

"We need a team meeting. I need to know more about that house and its previous owners."

8

Jon stood at the front of the incident room as the team filed in one by one and took their seats, chatting idly between themselves.

Watching his colleagues talking easily and laughing at the occasional joke, he wondered if it said anything about them that they could act like this amidst such a terrible case. All of them were able to block out the hateful things they had to deal with, day after day, and talk easily with their fellow officers about the weather and what TV they watched the night before, but did that make them heartless, or uncaring?

The answer, in his mind at least, was no. He knew that he cared deeply about all the cases he took on, and the victims of these terrible crimes. The pain and suffering that these people went through was nightmarish.

But he knew the truth of it. He knew that for most, if not all, it was a coping mechanism. You learnt to block it out and close off that part of your mind. Because if you didn't, it would be a slow descent into madness and depression.

Their humour, as dark and close to the bone as it was, came from the same place. If you didn't learn to laugh and find humour in these dark places, then you were likely in for a rough time of it.

They were dealing with the dregs of society, the scum at the very bottom of the barrel, and it was imperative that they realised that the vast majority of the human race was not evil. They were good people just trying to live their lives. The murderers and kidnappers were very much in the minority, which was something to take solace in.

"How's the new house?" Rachel asked as she took her place at the table.

"Yeah, good thanks," Jon replied, wondering where she was going with this, and what smart comment was about to come his way. "Really good."

"So, you won't be coming back to sleep on my sofa?"

"Hopefully not."

"Shame. Eric misses seeing you walk around in your boxers."

And there it was, he thought.

"Well, if I'd known that, I would have popped over more regularly." Kate snickered.

"Why?" Rachel asked. "It's not a pretty sight. He's hardly Brad Pitt."

"Me thinks she doth protest too much," Dion said. "Go on, admit it, you loved it."

"Oh yeah, I loved it," she said, her voice laced with sarcasm. "It was the highlight of my day."

"I knew it."

"Should I be jealous?" Kate asked, raising an eyebrow.

"You're not missing much," Jon said.

"I'm not so sure. I think I might request a private viewing."

"Ho-ho," Dion hooted. "Since when did you become so thirsty?"

"Alright guys, that's enough fun and games," Jon said, raising his voice. "We really need to crack on. Now, the Woods case. Kate, would you bring us up to speed?"

"Sure," she replied and leant forward onto the table. "Earlier today, Leonard Woods, a resident of Newdigate with his wife and young child, was engaging in some home improvement, knocking down a wall between a back room and their kitchen. Upon breaking the wall open, he discovered at least one human corpse bagged up and stored inside the wall. He called us in. We have interviewed the family, and so far we have no reason to suspect that Mr Woods had anything to do with the deaths of the people found."

"This was in an internal wall?" Dion asked. "Aren't they like, one brick thick?"

"The property is an old, quirky cottage, and some of the walls are usually thick," Jon replied. "We think the wall in question was originally an outside wall, but an extra room was built on the back, turning it into an internal wall."

"The Woods bought the house roughly a year and a half ago," Kate continued, "and from what we know so far, the bodies look at least that age. We'll know more once the pathologist has had a look at them."

"So, who owned the house before them?" Rachel asked.

"That's one of our first lines of enquiry. The Woods apparently bought it off a man called Duncan, who inherited it from his mother, and who then rented it out. But this is all based on their memories so far, so we need to look into that and see what we can confirm. We need to know who owned it before the Woods, and if it was rented out, who was it rented to."

"Also," Jon added. "A neighbour called Evan, who seems to have an interest in the property, we need to know a little more about him too. He seems to have clashed with the Woods a few times and I think he has a link to the property."

"We'll get onto it," Nathan replied.

"Good," Jon said, as his phone vibrated. He checked the message. "Looks like the pathologist is ready for a chat."

"Great," Kate replied.

"I need to check in with the Super before we leave the station, though. Is he around?"

"I think he's in his office," Nathan said.

"Okay, thanks," Jon replied. "Don't want to give him any excuse to stick his nose in. Right, you all know what to do. Let's get going."

Leaving the incident room, Jon marched over to the Detective Superintendent's office and knocked on the door. He could see DSupt Ray Johnston inside, sitting at his desk.

"Come in," he called out.

Jon stepped inside and closed the door behind him. "Sir."

"Aaah, Jon. Sorry to call you in on your day off, but this case came in, and I thought it was right up your street."

"Of course, sir. Happy to help."

"Good to hear it," Ray replied with a smile, and Jon got the impression that he'd done this on more than just a whim. It felt to him like Ray was testing him, maybe checking his dedication to the job and the team. He'd done this on purpose, though, whatever the reason.

"So, some bodies were found in the walls of a house," he stated.

"That's right sir. We're looking into it now. We've interviewed the current owners of the house; it was the husband who found them. But I don't believe they had anything to do with the bodies."

"And you're sure about that, are you?"

Jon nodded. He felt it was important to look confident about this. "I am."

"Okay, good, then I'll leave it in your capable hands."

"Very good, sir."

"See that you bring this one to a close like you did the last one."

"We'll do our best, sir," he answered. It felt like the DSupt was looking for any excuse to shut this unit down and didn't like that Jon and his team had a good record so far. Well, he wasn't about to make it easy on Ray, if that's what he wanted.

"Oh, Jon," the Super said before he could make it out the door. "Any news on that escapee?"

"Terry Sims? No, nothing. He's gone to ground. We're keeping an eye out for him, and we have his picture circulating, but we have no leads on him right now." Admitting this grated on him. After having three successful cases on the unit, it annoyed him that there was nothing to report on Terry Sims. But he wouldn't give up, and felt sure that Kate wouldn't either.

"Okay. Thank you, Pilgrim."

Leaving the office behind, Jon found Kate waiting at her desk, and wandered over.

"How'd it go?"

"Alright. I think he just wants to make sure we know that he's watching us."

"Hmm. Yeah. He's making his presence felt. He doesn't like this unit, that's for sure."

"No, he does not. He'd shut us down in a hot minute if he could justify it."

"You think he'd go that far?"

"Why not? I'm fairly sure that's what the ACC has put him here for."

"Well, let's hope we can do a good job on this one too. Maybe we can show him what we can do and get him on our side."

"If we can turn him into an advocate for the unit, then that would certainly help."

"It might get the ACC off the unit's back, that's for sure."

"The Assistant Chief Constable only did this because we stepped on the toes of someone he looks up to."

"I think we did more than step on his toes," Kate said. She was right. Russell Hodges came out of that case poorer and with his reputation tarnished. Part of that was Sydney's, no... Ariadne's doing, but Russell might not see it quite that way, and ACC Ward almost certainly did not. To him, he and Kate had threatened someone Ward looked up to, and taken him down a peg or two.

"Yeah," Jon remarked, his mind returning to Ariadne's appearance on his doorstep this morning. The memory tied his stomach in knots, and he wondered if she'd show up again soon.

The chances were high, he reasoned. She was up to something. He wasn't sure what, but it would probably be wise for him to be on his guard.

For a moment, he considered telling Kate about it, but he wasn't sure the time was right, and he didn't really know how to start.

"So, we're off to see Aileen, right?" Kate asked, and at that, the moment was gone. He decided to see how this Ariadne thing played out before he started telling anyone.

"Right," Jon replied as Kate gathered her things.

"You know, I've been thinking, and I've heard of this kind of thing before, you know? Bodies in walls, it's a gang thing. A way of disposing of their victims."

"You think there might be an organised crime element to this?"

"It would fit the evidence."

"Alright," Kate replied, as they made their way out. "I'd not thought about that. I thought it would be a serial killer."

"Might still be," Jon remarked. "I'm just spitballing here."

"Alright, well, we'll see, I suppose."

"We certainly will."

9

"So, have you come across this kind of thing before?" Kate asked as they approached the Mortuary. "Bodies in walls, I mean? Have you any experience with it?"

"No, not directly. But I've heard of it being used all over the world. Violent organised crime tends to leave a trail of bodies, and they need to be dealt with. I think they've just had to become inventive about how they hide them."

"How lovely," Kate muttered.

"I know. It's pretty grim stuff."

"Do you think this might be that then? You think there's a gang element to this?"

"Honestly, I've no idea. We just need to keep our options open, I think. We've skirted the edges of gang activity before, with the Russian Bratva and the Millers."

"Yeah," Kate mused. "Me too, with the cases I took on with Nathan, before you joined. Terry Sims was part of that."

"Yeah, I remember you saying. Ray asked about Terry when I went to see him."

"Did he now, okay," Kate said. "If we don't get anything on him soon, that could become an issue."

"I know. But he's just disappeared, and no one's talking."

"Someone will, and I can't believe that Terry will stay in hiding for too long. Someone knows something, and when they come forward, we need to be ready for it."

"We will be," Jon replied, confident.

"Did you have any plans for later, other than some more unpacking?"

"No, just that. I've got loads to do around the house."

"I thought so," Kate said.

"You?" Jon wondered if she'd been leading to something with her comment.

"Not much, no. I need to go shopping, I guess. I need to get some food in. But, part of me just wants to get a takeaway and worry about the food later."

"Hmm," Jon mused. The idea of a takeaway sounded divine. He could just go for something like that. "Sounds like a good idea to me."

"I know, right," she said, opening the door to the Mortuary. Moving inside, they found a thin, bespectacled man standing behind the desk with a clipboard. He was scribbling something down and looked up as they walked in.

"Uh, hello?"

"Hiya," Jon replied.

"Hello," Kate said. "We're here to see Aileen?"

"On what business?" the young man asked, pushing his glasses up on his nose. Jon guessed he was new and checked his name badge. Ben Hall, it read.

"Police business," Jon offered.

"Oh," Ben replied, looking a little surprised. "Oh, right. Jon and, um, Kate, right?"

"Got it in one, son."

"DCI Pilgrim, and DS O'Connell, actually," Kate said, sounding like a disapproving school teacher.

"Of course, yes. Sorry. She's, um, through here," he said, and led them through to the main examination room, where Aileen stood near one of the slabs. Jon counted eight occupied slabs, with bodies in a wide range of states, from just a collection of bones, to a couple of well preserved, but mummified ones.

"Busy day?" Jon asked.

"Aye, something like that," Aileen replied in her Scottish brogue.

"How many cases are you dealing with today? Looks like a few," Jon remarked, looking over the various remains.

"Just one," Aileen replied. "These all came from your house of horrors."

Jon felt his stomach drop as he realised what he was looking at and how many bodies had been stuffed into the walls at the Woods house.

"Oh, shite," Kate blurted out.

"You took the words right out of my mouth," Jon said. "So, there were eight bodies in that wall?"

"That's right," Aileen replied. "All of them had been bagged up, like the first." She pointed to the closest mummified one. "But not all of them were airtight, and some of them had already started to decay before they were sealed up."

"Okay, let's go from the top. What do we have?"

"Alright," Aileen replied. "Two of the eight were almost perfectly mummified. They were bagged very shortly after their deaths, and the bags were airtight. But these others are all in advanced states of decomposition. I think, based on the cursory examination I've been able to do so far, they were killed and left to decompose for a while before they were bagged and hidden."

"Okay," Jon replied. "You said they were killed. So, if they were murdered, do we know how?"

"I think I have a pretty good idea of that too. These remains, these bones are in good condition. There's one that has what looks like scrapes, most likely caused by a knife, though."

"So they were stabbed?"

"Actually, I think that was an anomaly. Maybe that one struggled more and took more subduing. The one commonality I found amongst almost all of them was a broken Hyoid bone. It's a small bone in the neck that often breaks from strangulation."

"They were strangled," Kate said.

"Do we know the genders of them? Ages?" Jon asked.

"I can make some estimates on age at this point, but nothing too precise. What I can say is that we have a mix of men and women in here. Three women and five men, actually, and I think they were mostly young adults."

"Anything else?"

"We have a few items that were found in the bags, which I've sent to forensics, and I've also sent some samples for DNA sequencing to see what we can get."

"Excellent, let's keep our fingers crossed," Jon replied. "Alright, so we have eight victims, men and women, all adults and all strangled."

"That sounds more like the work of a serial killer than organised crime," Kate remarked.

Jon shrugged. "I don't know. Maybe. You said one looked like it had been stabbed, right?"

"That's right," Aileen confirmed. "It's possible the others were too. Some of them, at least. If the knife didn't hit a bone on the six decomposed ones, we'd never know if they were stabbed or not."

"Fair point," Jon replied. "What about timeline? When were they killed?"

"Based on rate of decay between the mummified ones and the others, I think we're looking at around two to three years. One or two might be a touch longer, but it's hard to say at this point. I'll probably know more later."

"Thanks. That's a good start though, I can work with that." He looked back at Kate. "I still think there could be a gang angle to this. Strangulation doesn't rule that out for me."

"Alright," Kate answered. "I guess we'll see."

"I'm not taking bets on it, though."

"So not that confident in your theory then."

"I'm yet to plant my flag on either side," Jon explained. He was keeping his options open until he had more information at his disposal. It was just too early to know. As he thought through the new information, and what it meant for the investigation, his phone buzzed in his pocket.

Noting it was from the station, he turned away and took the call.

"Pilgrim."

"Jon," Rachel said on the other end of the line. "We've been doing some digging, and the man who owned the house before the Woods was Duncan Reid. He rented it out for a while, but we don't have a name on that front yet. Anyway, we've confirmed that Duncan inherited the house from his mother when she passed. Not only that, but it turns out that Duncan is the brother of Evan, the man the Woods have been having a little trouble with."

"Aaah, interesting, that explains his interest in the property then if he grew up in it."

"That was my conclusion too. Anyway, we have an address for him, which I'm emailing over now."

"Good work. I think Kate and I will pay him a little visit, see what he has to say for himself."

"Sounds good, boss," Rachel said and ended the call.

"Anything good?" Kate asked.

10

From Guildford, Jon drove south and made for Shackleford and a house just outside the village.

The weather had been good. It was nearing summer, and the temperatures had been increasing. It was pushing well into the mid-twenties, and as Jon drove out of the city, into the surrounding countryside with the windows down and the sun on his arm, it was easy to forget the horrors they were investigating.

Jon wasn't the biggest fan of hot weather and had never been one for soaking up the sun, but he'd begun to notice that things were, generally speaking, a lot warmer down here than they were back up in Nottingham.

He often found himself checking the difference between the weather down here and how many degrees cooler it was back up north. The difference was surprising.

Beside him, Kate had already removed her jacket and sat slumped in the car.

"Do you like the sun?"

"Me? Well, I have a kind of love-hate relationship with it, really. On the one hand, I always prefer the warmer weather. I like it hot. I much prefer that to the cold. But, my skin generally doesn't agree with me. I've always been pale, which is probably the Irish in me, and I tend to burn easily."

"Suncream it is then."

"Yeah. Factor fifty all the way, when I remember. I usually just end up looking like a lobster before I get into the habit of putting it on in the morning."

"Mmm, sexy."

Kate raised an eyebrow at him. "What are you, Spongebob or something?"

Jon went to speak, but then closed his mouth as he frowned at Kate's comment before he finally spoke. "I'm not sure that makes sense."

"Whatever, you big freak."

Jon turned into the address he'd been sent from the station. The house itself was a modest but nice detached affair, with a couple of outbuildings dotted around the good-sized garden. There were a few vehicles parked on the grounds, several cars, a van, and even an older motorcycle that looked like it had seen better days. The grass looked like it needed a cut around a couple of the cars, too. It looked like it was slowly consuming them.

"Someone isn't a gardener," Jon remarked as he saw a man wander out of what looked like a garage. He was wiping his hands on a rag and watched their unmarked car as Jon turned off the engine.

"Let's go and introduce ourselves, shall we?"

"I think that's a good idea. It might look weird if we just sit here staring at him."

"Good point, well made, Barry."

Kate smiled, as they both climbed out. Jon pulled his warrant card from his pocket as he approached.

"Can I help you?" the man asked.

"Yes," Jon replied, and held his card up. "I'm DCI Pilgrim. We're looking for Duncan Reid."

"You're speaking to him."

"Oh good. Can we have a moment of your time?"

"Yeah, sure. I guess. What's this about?"

"We need to ask you some questions, that's all," Kate said.

"Fair enough. Why don't we take a seat." He waved towards a set of metal garden chairs around a similar metal table and took one for himself. Jon followed suit, with Kate moving a chair to sit closer to him. "How can I help?"

"Well, firstly, I hope we're not interrupting anything?" Kate asked.

"Nothing of vital importance, no."

"Do you live alone here?"

"I do."

"And this is your house?" Jon asked.

"It is. I've lived here for years."

"Okay. We understand you used to own a house in Newdigate, is that right?"

"Yeah, Hill View, just off Rusper Road. My childhood home, actually."

"I see. And when did you own it from?"

"Well, I sold it about a year and a half ago, and I think I owned it for maybe a couple of years before that? Something like that, anyway. I didn't live there though, I just rented it out. I mean, I used to live there, when I was a child, like. It was my mother's house. But I'd moved out here, and when I inherited it, I didn't really want to live there, you know? So I thought it might be a good way to make a bit of money."

"And was it not? Is that why you sold it?"

"It was a lot of hassle, is what it was. I'd get called out to deal with stuff at all hours, and I just got fed up."

"And you sold it to the Woods family."

"I think so. Is that their name?"

Jon nodded.

"Alright then, if you say so."

"What about your brother? Were you not tempted to let him have it?"

"Evan? Nah, screw him. He's been nothing but a pain in my arse since he got back."

Jon frowned, wondering what that was all about, but he was getting a little ahead of himself and needed to go back to

80

the renting. "Okay, well, let's go back to the renting. How many tenants did you have during those two years?"

"Just the one."

"Aaaand, that was?"

"Oh. Corey Grant. He rented it from me for that whole time."

"I see," Jon replied. "And who is he?"

"Just a guy. I'd met him before a few times, and he said he needed a place to live. So, I offered the house, said he could rent it from me."

"So, he was a friend?"

"Yeah, I guess you could say that."

"And, what did Corey do, for a job I mean?"

"Aww, bits of this and that. He was a bit of a handyman I think. A jack of all trades. We didn't talk about it much. He didn't like to."

"Okay. So during those few years when Corey was renting it from you, did you do any work on the house? Any renovating? Build some walls, maybe?"

"Corey did," Duncan replied.

"Oh," Jon replied, and a jigsaw piece fell into place in his head. "Really? Isn't that a little unusual?"

"Nah, it was fine. He asked if he could, so we talked about it, and I let him do some re-wiring and stuff. He wasn't very good at it, though. He learnt it in prison, I think. You know, one of those schemes they do to try and get them working again."

"He'd spent some time in prison?" Kate asked.

"Some, yes. He could get angry, sometimes, and violent. He said he hurt someone and got sent down for it. He didn't like to talk about that either. But the building work, that's how he kept calm. He said he found it soothing."

"I see. And, did he do any work in the back room?"

"Aww yeah. He did a few bits back there, I think."

Jon nodded, catching a glance from Kate. He met her eyes briefly, and there was a mutual understanding that they knew they were onto something here.

"Great, so, he did some work for you, and then presumably moved out?"

"That's right," Duncan replied, and then he sighed. "It wasn't a good ending really. We argued, and he ended up moving out. That was the last straw for me, and that's when I sold the place."

"I see. And did you notice anything odd while he was living there? Any odd habits?"

"I'm not sure what you mean."

"It's hard to describe, but did you get the feeling he was keeping things from you?"

Duncan sighed. "A bit. He kept odd hours and didn't seem to work to any kind of schedule, I suppose. I'm not sure what he was doing. That was one of the things we argued about, actually."

"Did you keep in touch after he moved out?" Kate asked.

"Not really, no."

"Did he leave a forwarding address?" she pressed.

"No. He wasn't very happy with me. We had some issues, and I don't think he wanted to deal with them. So no, I don't know where he went."

"Okay, that's very helpful," Kate said.

"Let's return to Evan, then," Jon suggested. "You said he came back, so I take it he left?"

"Yep, he joined the army, leaving us. I was glad to see him go, to be honest. We fought a lot."

"Where was your father?"

"He left. That was what made Evan so angry. He hated that Dad just disappeared. Evan was away for years and never showed any interest in mum or me, and then just a few years ago, he shows up out of nowhere after mum died. He'd heard about her passing and that prompted him to come back here. Oh, he hated that I got the house and was renting it out. Hated it. But where was he when we needed him? When mum needed him? Nowhere, that's where. He's just been causing problems ever since."

Jon wondered if there might be some lingering issues from his time serving the country. Some PTSD maybe? He'd seen what it could do to some people if it wasn't treated and wondered if that was an issue here.

"So, was Evan around while Corey was renting from you?" Kate asked.

"Oh, yeah. He was causing problems back then, with Corey, showing up unannounced at the house and stuff. And then he tried to buy it when I sold it, but he didn't quite have the funds and lost out. Has he been causing problems for the family that's in there now? Is that what this is about?"

"It might be related," Jon admitted. "So, you don't have much contact with Evan?"

"Not really, no. We don't have much in common."

"And, other than the family connection, do you know why he might be interested in the house as much as he is?"

"Not really, no. I think it's just the family connection to it."

Jon nodded, but wasn't sure he agreed.

11

"Alright, here we are." Kate led Jon in through the front door of the apartment block. She smiled as he walked in and manoeuvred around him to close the door. As he waited, the door on his right to flat one opened, revealing an older woman with grey hair peering out.

"Oh, Kate dear, it's you. How are you?"

"Hi Francine," Kate replied, sounding a little exasperated that she'd appeared.

"Is this a friend of yours, dear? Are you going to introduce me?"

"Forgive Kate's rudeness," Jon cut in before Kate could say anything. "I'm Jon."

"Nice to meet you, Jon," Francine replied. Behind her, Kate pulled a face.

"And you, Francine. It's a pleasure. Kate has mentioned many times how much she enjoys your monthly residents' meetings." From the corner of his eyes, he could see Kate's shocked look. She mouthed the word 'no' as she drew her hand across her neck.

"Oh, thank you. I do enjoy putting them on. It's nice to know who you're living with, you know?"

"Well, I'll do my best to make sure Kate gets time off to attend."

Kate rolled her eyes, out of view of Francine.

"Oh, so you're her boss?"

"She works on my team, yes."

"How nice! That's a lovely accent you have, by the way. Are you not from around here?"

Jon smiled warmly at her. "Why, thank you. I'm so glad you like it." He gave Kate a look. She raised an eyebrow. "I'm from Nottingham, but I moved down for the job."

"That's dedication," Francine replied. "You must be a hard worker."

"I put the hours in," Jon answered, as Kate used her hands to indicate a swelling head.

"That's good to know. Well, I mustn't keep you. I'm not sure I would have been allowed to bring boys home with me when I was young, you know. But times change."

"Now Francine, you can't fool me. I'm sure you were a firecracker in your day."

"Oh tosh." She swatted at him with her hand. "You kids go and have fun. Goodbye Kate. You look after this one."

"I will. Bye Francine," Kate replied and smiled sweetly as Francine retreated to her room. With her gone, Kate's face turned to thunder as she waved her hand at him. "Go on, up you go. Jesus, what was that? You want me to attend more residents' meetings? Do you want my brain to turn to mush?"

"I was messin'," Jon replied with a smirk.

"She'll take it seriously, you know."

"I'm sure she will. Maybe I'll let you go to them more frequently. It's good to know your neighbours."

"Ugh. I know. But the meetings are so boring and awkward," she replied as they approached her door upstairs. "I'd rather be on a case."

"Fair enough. Let's get inside and have some food. I'm looking forward to this," he said, holding up the white carrier bag with the takeaway food inside. He could smell the inviting aroma coming from it, and couldn't wait to tuck in.

Kate led him inside. He placed the bag on the counter and set to work, pulling out the various boxes, while Kate busied herself with plates and drinks.

Within moments, they were sitting at the small, two-person table against the wall as Jon opened up the box of barbeque chicken wings he'd got from Royal Chicken in Leatherhead.

"They look messy," Kate said, picking up a slice of her pizza.

"They look divine," his mouth already watering at the thought of taking a bite. Without waiting another moment, he picked one up. It was still red hot from being packed in the box in foil wrap, and it took him a couple of tries to pull the first wing free from the others and take a bite.

But the moment he did, it was as if he'd gone to heaven.

The BBQ sauce was simply wonderful. He quickly forgot that his fingertips were being slowly seared by the heat from the wing as he devoured the tasty treat and moved onto the next one.

They were messy, for sure, and within moments his fingers were covered in BBQ sauce. He felt sure he had it all around his mouth too. It probably wasn't good date food really, and it perhaps didn't make a great impression, but Kate knew him well enough by now, so if she was put off by some messy food, well, that was on her.

Besides, this wasn't just food. This was manna from the very gods themselves. This was mind-expanding wondrousness. Was that even a word? He didn't care.

All he cared about was getting another bite of chicken in his mouth. Right freaking now.

"Wow, you really like that, don't you," Kate said, plucking a chip from his plate.

"Oi! Get your own chips if you want some."

"But, I don't want a full portion. Besides, if you loved me, you wouldn't mind."

"I'm gonna go off you pretty quick if you keep stealing my food."

"You don't mean that," she said and reached for another chip.

He swatted at her hand and got some sauce on her fingers.

"Ack! Hey, look what you did." With a sigh, she popped a finger in her mouth and sucked the sauce off. The moment she did, her eyes bugged, she stared at him. "Oh wow, now that is special."

"I know," he replied and covered the box of chicken with his hands. "And they're mine."

"You can spare one, surely. You can have some of my pizza."

"Get your own."

"Oh, please! Just one. I just want to try one. That's a lot of chicken you have there."

Jon sighed, knowing he'd never hear the end of it if he didn't. "Okay, fine," he said, and pulled out a wing. "Here you go."

"Thank you," she said with a smile and bit into it. "Mmm, mmm, that is amazing."

"Messy, but worth it," Jon replied.

"So worth it," Kate agreed, sauce already around her mouth. "So very worth it."

Jon tucked into the rest of his food. A short time and a quick hand wash later, he sat sideways in his chair with his back against the wall, and a can of fizzy drink in his hand, feeling suitably stuffed. Kate did likewise.

"I'm sure I'm going to regret this later," she said.

"Me too, but I just don't care. I'd eat that again tomorrow, and the next day, and the next day…"

"Well, I know what I'll be having the next time I go there."

"Have you been there before?"

"Yeah. They're fairly close so…"

"Convenient."

"Yep."

"Any thoughts on the case, so far?" he asked, taking a sip of his drink.

"I don't know. Duncan seems credible, and he didn't live in the house during the time that the bodies were placed there. I'm curious to know more about this Corey Grant."

"Me too," Jon agreed. "I have a feeling he might have some secrets for us."

"Secrets?"

"I'm just going on what Duncan said. No set work hours, late nights, didn't want to talk about his job, and prison time. I think he was up to no good."

"Since he's been in prison, then we'll have a look at his record. This might be the gang connection you talked about."

"Right. And if it is, he's just booked himself a place at the number one spot on our suspect list."

"Lucky him."

"Well, we'll see what tomorrow brings."

"Yep. So, do you want to stay the night?"

Jon considered his options. "Tempting," he replied.

"You've got a better offer?"

"No. It's just that it's not too late, and I can get a couple of hours of unpacking done if I get home before hitting the sack."

"Yeah, fair enough. I was surprised you came and had dinner with me."

"I could hardly say no to that offer. And I'm glad I didn't because that was delicious."

"It was," Kate agreed. "So, you're heading back to Guildford then?"

"If that's okay? I don't like just disappearing given how little time we get to ourselves, but I'm desperate to get the house liveable as soon as possible."

"I'd offer to come with you, but I'm in a mess here, and I might go and do some late night shopping, anyway," Kate replied.

"That's fine. You can help another time. Give the place a woman's touch."

Kate wiggled her eyebrows at him. "Glad to. We wouldn't want it becoming too much of a man-cave. You might scare us little ladies off."

"And I wouldn't want that," he replied.

Saying his goodbyes, he drove back west to Guildford and his home. It wasn't too late, and he was keen to do something constructive before he dived into bed. If he procrastinated, he'd get nothing done, and he'd end up living out of boxes, something he really didn't want to do.

Walking up to his house, he turned into the front path through the modest front garden and stopped dead in his tracks.

Ariadne was sitting on his front step, a bottle of champagne in her hand.

"Surprise," she said with a smile.

Jon sighed, loudly, and put his weight on one leg. "What are you doing here?"

She got to her feet. "I realised I didn't bring you a moving-in gift, so I thought I'd rectify that oversight." She waved the bottle around before her.

"I see. And after our little chat this morning, you thought that I wanted to see you again, did you?"

"Jon. You're being rude again."

Jon rolled his eyes. Admittedly she was right, and although she was clearly a Black Widow of sorts, she'd actually been nothing but nice to him. Too nice really, and a little too affectionate. But there was a dangerous side to her, of that he was certain.

"Okay, sure," he replied, thinking that he'd play along for a while, to see where this went. "I'll play nice."

"Well, that's a start, at least. May I come in?"

"I don't think that's such a great idea, Ariadne. I said I'd be civil, but that doesn't mean inviting you in for a drink when my girlfriend isn't here."

Now she sighed. "And here I was, thinking we were just starting to get along."

"Sorry to disappoint you," Jon replied.

"You don't disappoint me, Jon. You could never do that."

"I beg to differ, but okay."

"Here, this is yours. I was hoping to share it with you," she said. It was curious. Her tone had changed, she sounded a little more normal and a little less like she was trying to seduce him. Although that in itself could be a clever tactic on her part to try and woo him. That and the bottle of bubbly.

"So, how is your beautiful girlfriend? Kate, right?"

"DS O'Connell to you."

She gave him a look.

He sighed, and nodded. "She's fine. We're fine, thank you. Great, actually."

"How wonderful for you," she said, sounding a little more like her usual sultry self.

"Oi, Pilgrim, you fucker." Jon looked up at a passing van. A man leant out of the window, hollering at him as it passed at a slow, rolling pace. "You and Kate better watch yourselves, you know, wouldn't want either of you getting hurt, if you know what I mean."

The man laughed, and the van sped off down the street. Jon watched it go, shocked that anyone knew who he was and where he lived. After a moment, he realised he'd forgotten to get the number plate, and made to run for the road. He slowed and never got there. It was too late, and the van was too far off.

"Shit," he cursed.

"What the hell was that?" Ariadne asked.

Jon watched the van, way in the distance, turn a corner and disappear from sight. He shook his head. "I have no idea."

"Have you pissed someone off recently?"

Jon gave Ariadne a look. "I'm a police officer. I piss people off all the time. You should know that better than most."

"Of course you do. Hmm, well, looks like someone knows where you live."

"The thought had occurred to me," Jon said, feeling a little worried. He made a mental note to get some stronger locks installed as he wondered who the man was. As he stared off into the distance, he remembered seeing a man standing outside the house last night after he moved in. Was that the same man?

Had he been watching him? It made sense. Damn it. He'd need to keep an eye out when he came home from now on, just in case.

"So, how about that drink, Jon?"

He returned his attention to Ariadne and raised an eyebrow again. "Sorry, no. I've got some jobs to do. But thank you for the gift, I appreciate it."

"Well, at least you were polite to me this time. That's a start, I guess."

Jon shrugged. He didn't see the point in being rude, provided she wasn't overstepping the mark.

"I'll see you around, Jon."

He watched her go, all hips and heels. She climbed into a totally different car this time and was gone in short order, leaving him to enter his house alone. Out of curiosity, he looked up the champagne she'd given him online and nearly had a heart attack at the price tag.

Suddenly, he wasn't sure if he should drink it or sell it.

12

How long had it been?

Hours? Days? Helen had lost all track of time and couldn't be sure how long she'd been in here. The light coming from the vent had never changed, meaning it was likely artificial, giving her no clue as to what time of day it was.

Her stomach grumbled loudly again, making her insides cramp.

In some ways, it was nice to have a new, different pain to focus on. Her wrists ached endlessly, but she'd somehow started to get used to it... until she moved them, and the tight, lancing pain flared again.

Her legs felt like jelly, and if it wasn't for her being wedged between these two walls, she would have fallen over ages ago.

The hunger she felt was painful, but it was beaten easily by her intense thirst. Helen's mouth was bone dry, and her tongue felt like sandpaper as she leant her head against the wall before her. It wasn't brick. She'd realised this a while back. The wall at her back was brick, but the one in front was very clearly wood.

Not that it mattered. She wasn't in a position to do much of anything. Shouting or banging on the wall with her head, or foot, or knee, only resulted in more pain.

Sometimes that pain was welcome, and other times it wasn't.

She'd been drifting in and out of sleep for a while and had started to lose some grip on what was real and what was a dream. It was no doubt dehydration kicking in as her body tried to conserve its water and keep her alive.

How long did she have? A few days, maybe? If only she could make someone aware she was missing, maybe then someone might start looking for her.

But she'd not told anyone where she was going, and she had no idea where her phone was.

Thinking was becoming tiring, and she felt shattered. Helen closed her eyes, hoping some rest would help, and drifted into another dark and fitful sleep, filled with nightmarish dreams.

13

Jon settled into his office chair as he booted up his PC. As he sat there, his mind couldn't help returning to the night before and the events that had taken place at his doorstep.

Ariadne turning up again was disturbing enough on its own, and he didn't like that she was apparently making an effort to insert herself into his life for a second time.

He still didn't know what she was really up to, but there had to be a reason. He couldn't quite believe that she just wanted to be his friend and hang out. That just didn't seem right to him at all and didn't fit with who she was. This was a woman who had no issues seducing a man and becoming his girlfriend for at least a few months before swindling and stealing millions from him.

She was focused, dedicated and calculating, and he found it hard to believe she'd do this without a deeper, hidden meaning. But what was it, and why?

What was her end goal?

He had a sinking feeling that he probably wouldn't know until it was too late, and he'd already stepped willingly into her trap.

But that wasn't even the most disturbing thing to happen last night. He found himself thinking back to that passing van as he tried to picture it in his mind's eye. He'd not got a good look at the man or even really seen the number plate, but that didn't stop him from trying to focus on those details and try to pull something from his memories. Something he could enter into the police database and get some kind of lead or clue.

But so far, his luck had failed him.

He'd been thinking about it all last night as he unpacked a few more boxes, and inevitably he'd got less done because his mind was not on the job at hand.

In the end, he went to bed late after checking the locks several times and jamming a chair under the door. But sleep had been a fickle mistress and ended up eluding him for half the night as his mind raced with thoughts, questions, and fears.

In the end, he came into work early and was the first one in.

As the computer finished booting up, he started to look back over the last three cases and the people they'd charged and wondered if it might be related to any of them. Was it linked to the Millers or the Russians? They were probably the most likely choices, and yet, either they'd escaped punishment altogether in the Miller case, or they'd been sent down in the case of Vassili, with little chance of them getting out any time soon.

That might not stop him from ordering someone to torment him, though. Someone like Vassili probably had friends who were more than willing to do jobs for him.

The thought was a worrying one, for sure.

But it might not be Vassili. It could just as easily be Abban or his son issuing those orders, or friends of Blake, or even Russell.

Jon sighed as he buried his face in his hands after spending far too long going through the case files on the system.

"You look tired."

Looking up, Jon met Kate's eyes as she smiled at him from the doorway, holding drinks.

"Hey. Yeah, I am tired."

"Bad night's sleep?"

"You could say that."

"Anything I can help with?" she asked as she placed a mug of tea down on his desk.

"I don't know about helping, but you should certainly know about it because it concerns you too."

"Oh?" Kate asked.

"I was threatened last night."

"Oh! Really? Crap. What happened?" she asked, a concerned expression on her face. Given her past with Abban, he wasn't the biggest fan of dropping this news on her. The last thing either of them needed was another criminal taking a personal interest in them again.

"A van drove past as I was about to enter my house, and a man shouted at me. He said that you and I should be careful. Otherwise, we might get hurt."

"He said my name?"

Jon nodded. "He did, and he knows where I live."

"Shite, that's not good."

"No. I've been awake all night thinking about it. This morning I've been going through the database to see if I can see anything. It wasn't much use though, I've got nothing but half baked theories and ideas. It could be coming from anyone, even someone from up north who's followed me down here. I've pissed off a lot of people in my time."

"Likewise," Kate agreed. "Okay, if you come up with anything, any ideas, or if anything else happens, let me know, okay? I'll see if I can find anything too."

"Thanks, Kate. You're a star."

"No problem. I'm doing this to save my arse, too, you know."

"Good, I don't want to see anything bad happen to your arse."

She smirked. "It's a good thing we're dating, matey. I could have you for sexual harassment."

Jon felt two-foot-tall suddenly as he realised what he'd said. "Yeah, sorry."

She laughed. "Hey, it's okay, I don't mind. I know you wouldn't do anything if we weren't dating. It's cute coming from you. I'm glad you hold my ass in high regard."

"The highest, I'd put it on a pedestal and worship it if I could."

"Now you're just getting weird," she replied, screwing her face up. "Drink your tea. I'll organise a team meeting, yeah?"

"Yeah, thanks, that would be great."

"On it," she replied with a wink and left the room.

A short time later, Jon joined the rest of the SIU at the table in the Incident room, aware that he probably looked a little rough around the edges. He didn't care too much and focused his mind on the case at hand.

"Alright, where are we?"

"The incident room, sir," Dion replied. "Are you sure you're alright?"

"Shut it, smart arse," Jon replied with an eye roll.

"Shutting it, guv."

"Anyone care to answer without a smart-alec remark?"

"I looked into Corey Grant, Duncan's tenant," Nathan said. "He did indeed serve time in High Down Prison, as Duncan said. He was convicted on several counts of GBH, ABH and Affray, as well as some other things. It turns out that Corey is quite a violent man. And not only that, but he has some links to the Miller crime family too."

"Links?" Jon replied.

"The details on this are sketchy," Nathan replied. "But he's been seen with at least two core members of the Miller gang. Brent Miller and Dillon Harris. He's pulled jobs with them before, and we have witnesses to attest to that. As for how close he was to the gang, and if he's still associated with them, I have no idea."

"Okay," Jon replied. "That's great work. I think he's someone we should speak to."

"And that's where you might run into problems," Nathan replied.

"How come?"

"We have no permanent address for him following his departure from Duncan's place, and little else on the record. I can tell you that I don't think he's left the country, but even that's not concrete. I can't believe I'm going to say this, but I've got no idea where he is."

"You're right. I don't believe it. There must be something. I want to know his previous addresses, the people he knew, everything. There must be something that will give us some clue as to where he is. I think we need to speak to Brent and Dillon too. They might know where he is. Nathan, you take Dillon, I'll take Brent."

"Will do, guv. And I'll keep hunting."

"Good, thanks. What else do we have?"

"I've been taking a closer look at Evan," Rachel said, leaning forward. "Duncan was telling the truth. Evan served in the military for years, taking in several tours of some pretty shitty places. He's been in the thick of it, and according to his record, he's lost several colleagues along the way."

"So some PTSD is not unlikely," Jon guessed.

"It's not just likely, it's confirmed. He's had some psychological treatment, and he's taken some meds over the years. He struggled with anger issues, and he seems to fixate on things too."

"Like the house," Jon replied.

"As you say," Rachel replied with a nod. "The Woods have reported him to us several times over the year and a half they've been there, but not much was ever really done about it, apart from warning Evan about his behaviour. It seems like he always ends up going back to his usual ways, though."

"A neighbour from hell," Kate said.

"Yep," Rachel agreed.

"He's a big man too," Kate added. "Not someone I'd like banging on my door and getting angry at me."

"The Woods said several times in statements that they feared he might become violent."

Jon nodded and sighed. "Okay, well, we know he used to live at that house, so he has a strong personal connection to it, and with his mother dead and his father missing, that house probably represents the only link he has to his past. That alone is likely to be enough to trigger someone with a psyche as fragile as his if the current owners start to make changes to it."

"He sees them as defiling not only his home," Kate said, "but his past, his family and him. It's incredibly personal to him."

"Agreed," Jon replied. "But does he have anything to do with the bodies that were found in the house?"

Rachel sat back and shrugged. "I don't know. He was around when Corey was there, too, although he never reported him."

"If Corey is a violent criminal, I think 'A' he can handle himself, and 'B' he probably doesn't want the police anywhere near his stuff. I don't see Corey being scared of Evan."

"True," Rachel said.

"And who knows, we're going off one person's word about Evan and Corey. These two seem like two peas in a pod to me. They come from different backgrounds, but they're both violent and possibly unstable people. Who's to say they weren't friends."

"You're suggesting they did this together?" Rachel asked.

"I'm just floating ideas out there."

"Throw enough shit at the wall, and some of it's bound to stick," Dion said.

"Eww," Rachel said, squirming.

"But we know that, according to Duncan, Corey did some work on the house, too," Kate said. "I don't think Evan would like him doing that. I'm not sure I can see these two working together."

"True," Jon replied. "But who's to say Evan didn't do it? Maybe he let his temper get the better of him, and he had some bodies to hide? I just don't want to shut off any possibilities. Okay, Dion, did you find anything out about Duncan?"

"Yeah. He's currently out of work, and I assume living off the proceeds of the house sale, but he used to work in an office job." Dion replied. "He left it after he started renting the house out. Then, after he sold it, Duncan switched sides and became a tenant himself."

"Oh?" Jon asked.

"Yeah, he rented a house in Redhill for about eight months from a woman called Polly Elliot. He stopped renting it about three months ago."

Jon frowned. "Why?"

"No idea," Dion said.

"Hmm, okay, well, there's no law against people owning one house and renting another. Still, look into it and get me a meeting with this Polly. She might be able to shed some light onto this for us."

"Will do, boss," Dion replied.

"Alright. What about these bodies? Do we have anything on them?"

"Not much," Nathan answered. "We've all been doing what we can, but it's a massive mountain to climb. People go missing all the time in the UK, and many are never reported or never found, so…"

"Yeah, it's like, two thousand people a year, isn't it? It's something crazy like that," Kate said.

"I've heard those stats too," Jon replied. "I know it's a huge task, but see what you can find. The pathologist said they sent some items to Forensics."

"They did," Nathan confirmed. "One was a phone, there was a pen and a wallet too. We might be lucky and get some hits on DNA too. I'll let you know if we get anything concrete."

"Perfect, thanks," Jon replied.

"So, what's next?" Kate asked.

"I want to see this Evan Reid first, and then we'll pay a visit to Brent Miller and see what we can scare up," Jon replied.

14

"I had a little hunt through the case files, looking for any known associates of Blake, Vassili, Russell, Abban and the others," Kate said as Jon drove them down to Newdigate and Evan's house.

Surrounded by the lush countryside on what looked like it might prove to be another warm day, it was difficult to believe there were vicious killers out there, stalking their prey.

But the realities of his job would come smashing onto his desk all too often to remind him that people could easily be massive shits and cause all kinds of harm to everyone around them.

"And, what did you find?" Jon asked, focusing on the road ahead as it wound through the idyllic landscape.

"You're not going to like it."

"Of course I'm not," Jon stated. "Let me guess, they all have friends who're a little dodgy and who'd happily do a little stalking on the side for their friends. Am I close?"

"Uncannily," Kate replied. "Although admittedly, it's not much of a surprise, I guess."

"Figures."

"Yeah. Some have more of these kinds of friends than others. Russell, for instance, is a little light on that front, but some of the others have contacts that would all too happily threaten you."

"Wonderful," Jon replied, meaning the exact opposite.

"I think we both just need to be careful," Kate said.

"Agreed. How do you want to do this? Do you want to stay at mine for a bit?"

"Not really."

"Oh?" Jon said, feeling a little surprised by her blunt answer.

"Don't take that the wrong way, but I've lived my life being tormented by a hidden killer. I'm kind of used to it, and besides, I failed to get to the supermarket last night, so I still need to go."

He couldn't help but chuckle at her irreverence. "No, you're right," Jon replied, taking a breath. "We can't let these idiots dictate how we live our lives, and I refuse to be cowed by a few threats."

"My thoughts exactly," Kate agreed. "Still, be a little careful. I don't want my cute little northerner's face getting beaten up."

"Cute little northerner?" Jon asked, eyebrows raised.

"What? You are!"

"I'm not sure I've ever been called cute... or little, before."

"It's the angle you're looking at it from. No man ever thinks they're small."

Jon snorted. "Maybe I should be reporting you to HR, Missy. Jesus. And hey, are you calling me small?"

"A woman never tells," Kate said, putting a superior expression on her face. "Unless it's my girly mates, I tell them everything."

"Shut it, you," Jon replied. "And you've still not answered my question."

"Do you need your ego stroking?"

"Yes," Jon replied, putting on a pout.

"Well... we're here, so it'll have to wait," Kate said, nodding out the front window.

"Tease," Jon accused her.

She winked. "If you want a piece of this ass you supposedly worship, you'll have to be patient."

"Christ, you're on fire today."

As Kate got out of the car, she licked her finger and touched her bum with it, making a hissing sound through her teeth.

Jon smirked as he got out and stepped onto the pavement. Pausing, he looked up at Evan's quite nice semi-detached house and then turned and looked up the street. Just a hundred yards or so away, he could make out the blue and white police tape strung up before the Woods' house. A single uniformed officer stood guard, his marked car close by.

"He's close to the Woods' house," Jon said.

"Very," Kate agreed, following his gaze. "Just a short walk.

"Hmm," Jon replied and took the lead. Walking up to the front door of the house, he rang the bell. Evan answered a short time later.

"Oh, Detectives," he said, obviously a little surprised.

"Well remembered," Jon said, unable to stop a little sarcasm slipping out. "I'm DCI Pilgrim, and this is Detective O'Connell."

"Okay. Do you want to come in?"

"If that's okay, we just want to talk."

"Yeah, fuck it, whatever."

Evan led them into the front room, an open-plan affair that went right through the house to the back, creating a lounge/diner. The furniture was sparse and functional. The only cluttered space was a dresser, covered in photos of people in camouflage, a beret, and several display frames with medals in them. It was impressive, he thought, as he caught Evan watching him. Jon took a seat beside Kate.

"This is about the house, right?" Evan asked from where he sat on the sofa. "I heard they found bodies in there?"

"It is."

"Am I a suspect?"

"You're just someone we need to speak to," Jon answered.

"Right," he replied, unimpressed. "Well go on then, shoot."

"It was your home, wasn't it?"

"That's right. Once," he replied, looking down and balling his fists. This seemed to be an emotional subject for him.

"And you want it to be again?" Jon asked.

Even let out a long breath. "Honestly, I don't know. Not now. I mean, I did, yeah. After mum died, I... I think it was the only connection I had to them."

"You went away, though, didn't you?"

"Yeah. I needed to. I couldn't stay there. I..." Evan took another long, steadying breath as Jon noticed his hands shaking. He balled his fists several times over. "I've spoken about this a lot with my shrink. I'm sorry but, it seems that I have some anger issues. I'm working through them, and I take medication but, I struggle with it."

"I understand," Jon replied. "Take your time."

"Thanks," he replied with a sigh. He attempted to calm himself, but Jon could see the anger beneath the surface, bubbling away, waiting to burst forth. "I went away, yes. I joined the army and travelled around. I was good at it. But when I heard that mum had died, I knew I had to come back. I needed to reconnect or something. I'm not sure I should ever have left in the first place and left my mum alone like that."

"And then you come back and find that your brother is renting the house out."

Evan stood up suddenly and kicked the small wooden coffee table, knocking it over.

Evan stalked to the nearby front window and put his head in his hands. "Sorry," he said, turning back to them. "But, he shouldn't have done that. I can't believe he did it. I hated... I found it difficult to deal with that he'd started renting it. It was our house, our mother's. We shouldn't be renting it out to any old shithead."

"I take it you're angry with Duncan for this?"

"Um yeah. I guess you could... Yeah, I have some issues there. That's what my shrink says, anyway—some unresolved issues. I need to deal with them, but then this happens. How am I supposed to get over this when this shit happens? Huh? How? Tell me that. Tell me how I'm supposed to deal with his fucking shit when bodies are found in my fucking mother's house?" He was shouting at them by the time he stopped.

"Calm down, Mr Reid," Jon said, raising his hands. He looked like he was about to break something or put his hand through a wall.

Evan took a deep breath. "I know, I'm sorry. I just get so angry."

"I understand. We don't have to do this now if you don't want."

"No, please. You need to ask your questions. Please, go on."

"Alright. Well, I can see you're upset with Duncan."

"Pissed fucking off, more like it."

Jon gave Evan a look.

"Sorry," Evan said.

"That's okay. Why are you upset at him?"

"It's the disrespect. Duncan doesn't care about the house, clearly. How could he if he rents it out and then sells it? It should have stayed in the family, it should have gone to me, and then maybe none of this shit would have happened."

"I see. But it didn't, did it? It got sold to the Woods family."

"Pompous, stuck up snobs. They think their shit don't stink. Well, I've got news for them, it does. Look at the fucking mess they're in now."

"You couldn't afford it, could you?"

"No," Evan confirmed. "It's all just money, money, money, these days isn't it? Duncan should have sold it to me. I'm supposed to be his brother, after all. I would have looked after it, kept it nice for mum. Instead, the Woods just want to butcher it, destroy it and turn it into something else. Well, look where that got them."

"Are you saying they deserved it?" Kate asked.

"I'm saying they shouldn't have gone changing things. That's our legacy, my mother's legacy, and they've defiled it."

"Okay, so do you know where the bodies came from? We found several in the walls of the house. The wall between the kitchen and the backroom, specifically."

Evan shrugged. "How should I know? I've got no idea how they ended up there."

"No idea at all?"

"Nope."

"Do you think it might have been your brother or his tenant? Or someone else?"

"Yeah, maybe. They'd fucking deserve it if it was, anyway. Serves them right. Fuck 'em."

"I see," Jon said, shocked by what Evan was telling them.

Later, in the car, Jon looked over at Kate. "He's a man on the edge."

"For a moment there, I thought he was going to attack us," Kate said. "He's got some serious anger issues."

"You're not kidding."

15

Jon wandered across the forecourt and into the main entrance of Miller Bodyworks, with Kate beside him. Men worked on cars all around them. Several looked up at the visitors.

Jon scanned the workshop, looking for Brent, but couldn't see him right away.

"Jon," Kate said.

He looked over, and Kate was pointing through a nearby window into a side office, where Brent sat at a desk on the phone, apparently oblivious to their entry.

"There you are," Jon muttered and set off towards the door. As they closed in, a man stepped in front of them, his hands up.

"Whoa, hold on there. Where do you think you're going?"

Jon frowned, making sure to look suitably confused. "In there," he said, pointing to the office behind him.

"You can't go in there."

"Why not?"

The man squared up to him, his expression hardening. "Because I said so, dick head."

Jon was about to reach for his warrant card when Kate shoved hers in his face.

"Oi, dick head," she barked. "Move it, or you get a free trip to the station."

"Oh, sorry," the man said and backed up.

"What's the matter?" Jon asked. "It's a lovely station. The cells are especially nice. Don't you want to see?"

"No, no. You're good," the man said, looking cautious. He hustled over to the office and poked his head inside. As Jon approached, he heard him speak to Brent. "Boss, the pigs are here, what do you want to do?"

Brent glanced through the window at them. He spoke into the phone and ended the call before speaking to the mechanic, his words lost in the noise of the garage. The man turned to Jon and Kate and opened the office door wider. "In you go," the mechanic said, watching them closely.

Jon nodded to him with a smug smile. As he walked through, he patted the man on the shoulder. "You did the right thing." Followed by Kate, who thanked him sweetly.

"Detectives," Brent said brightly, holding his hands wide. He remained seated, though. "And who do I have the pleasure of meeting today?"

"I'm DCI Pilgrim, this is DS O'Connell."

"Pilgrim and O'Connell. Right you are. What can I do for you this fine day? I don't believe I've done anything to cause such a visit."

"Nope," Jon replied. "*You* haven't."

"Oh good, that's what I like to hear. Please then, take a seat. I must say, you've taken me by surprise. I usually know if I'm going to get a visit from the local plods."

"I'm pleased to surprise you," Jon replied.

"I'm not," he said, a note of threat in his voice. After a moment's pause, he carried on in a lighter tone. "So, what can I do for Surrey's finest?"

"We were wondering if you might be able to tell us where a friend of yours is," Jon asked.

"A friend of mine? Well, that depends on the friend, but I'll certainly try," he replied, putting some mock effort into his voice.

Jon frowned at his blatant disrespect for the law, and them specifically. He was a Miller, after all, and one of the younger ones. He didn't look old enough to run a business like this, and that annoyed Jon. He was born into a life of privilege and crime, and likely as not, walked into this job without any worries at all. That felt wrong, but it was just the way things were.

Turning from the desk, Jon looked through the window into the workshop. Several of the men had stopped working and were standing in small groups, talking and glancing furtively at him and Kate. They were no doubt worried about their boss.

Jon grimaced and wondered how many of them had criminal records and were aware of what the Millers did? Several of them most likely.

"Nice place you have here," Jon said.

"Thanks. It does alright."

"Family business, is it?"

"Something like that," Brent replied. "Can I get you a drink, officers? Tea, coffee? Something stronger maybe? Rum? Brandy?"

"No thanks, Mr Miller," Kate replied, all business.

"As the lady says," Jon added.

"Well, I'm having one." Brent walked to a nearby drinks cabinet and poured himself a generous helping of what looked like whisky. "Are you sure I can't tempt you?"

"Not while I'm working," Jon answered.

"That's dedication to the job. I'm impressed."

"Really?" Jon replied, turning back to him. "That impressed you? Wow, you have low standards."

Brent's expression grew dark. "What can I do for you?"

"How's Dillon these days?" Jon asked. "And Irving? Are they well?"

"They're alright."

"Have you seen Dillon recently?"

Brent shrugged.

"What about Corey Grant?"

119

"I don't know."

"You don't know if you've seen Dillon and Corey recently? Well, I think you might need to go to the doctor. Looks like you've got a memory issue going on there. That's really not good in a man as young as you are. I think you should get that checked out."

"Yeah, that's really bad," Kate agreed. "Might be early onset Alzheimer's or something."

"I had a relative who had that," Jon continued. "Ended up not knowing what day of the week it was. It was all very sad. Sorry mate, the outlook doesn't look good."

"I ain't seen Corey in ages, alright?" Brent snapped. "I've got no idea where he is. Is that what you want to know?"

"You've not seen him in ages?"

"No."

"Ages? Is that a technical term I'm not aware of, Kate? Is that like weeks or months?"

"I don't know," Brent said, before Kate could reply. "Months maybe?"

"Months. Alright, that's helpful. Do you have a contact number for him or anything?"

"Nope," Brent replied.

"You're sure?"

"Quite sure."

"So, you're admitting that you know Corey, then. You worked with him, right?"

"I didn't say that," Brent answered, as he flushed, looking a little panicked. "I just said I've not seen him in a while. I don't really know him, not well, anyway. He's just a friend of a friend."

"Just a friend, I see. So you've not worked with him at all?"

"How? On what? Here, in the garage?"

"I don't know, maybe."

"I have no idea what you're going on about. You know what?" Brent asked. "I feel a phone call to Irving coming on. I think we should have a chat. He's quite friendly with some of the top brass in the Surrey police, you know."

Jon narrowed his eyes and leaned in. "You do that. See if I care."

"I think you might care, Mr Detective man."

"Wow, these insults are intense," Jon said. "I might not sleep tonight."

"I nearly wet myself with that last one," Kate agreed.

"Yeah, it gave me the willies."

"Have you got what you came here for, Pilgrim?"

"I think so," Jon replied as his phone buzzed once in his pocket. He pulled it out and checked the notification. It was from Nathan, who had apparently just got out of a meeting with Dillon Harris.

"Good day then, officers," Brent said, standing up. "We've got work to do, and I can't sit around talking to you all day."

"Quite," Jon said. "We'll be in touch if we need to speak to you again."

"Can't wait," Brent answered as he showed them out.

Jon and Kate were soon back at the car, where Jon pulled out his phone and started tapping. "Nathan messaged. I'll just give him a quick call."

Kate nodded as the call went through, and Nathan answered.

"Guv," Nathan said.

"How'd it go with Dillon?"

"How do you think? He was singularly unhelpful. About the only thing he did tell me was that he hasn't seen Corey in a while."

"Yeah, same for us," Jon replied. "He might be lying and just deflecting, but I can't say for sure."

"No, me neither. Okay, I'll see you back at the office."

"Will do," Jon said, and ended the call.

"He got nothing too?"

"Aye. Bugger all."

"Not very surprising, though, is it?"

"Not really," Jon agreed. "Right, what's next?"

16

"Mrs Polly Elliot, is it?" Jon asked the woman who answered the door.

She was short and a little stocky, wearing a business skirt and blouse with her hair tied up. He thought it was slightly odd clothing to wear around the house, but didn't think anything more of it. "Yes, how can I help you?"

Jon raised his warrant card. "I'm Detective Jon Pilgrim, Ma'am, and this is DS Kate O'Connell. We were wondering if we might speak to you regarding a case we're looking into."

"A case? What case? Should I be worried?"

"Hopefully not, Mrs Elliot, and you're not in any trouble. But you might know some useful information. Can we come in?"

"Sorry, yes, of course. Come in, please," she said and let them into the modest house on the outskirts of Redhill. Everything was well looked after in the garden outside, and the inside was equally clean and orderly. "Come through to, um... Let's go to the kitchen, I suppose. Can I get either of you a drink? I've just brewed up some tea."

"That would be lovely, thanks," Jon said as they followed her through to the kitchen at the back of the house, where she poured out two mugs and offered them milk and sugar.

"Are you sure you don't want to speak to my husband?"

"I don't know, maybe. Who deals with the houses you rent out?"

"Oh, that's me," she said. "My husband's a dentist. He doesn't have much to do with the houses. They're my thing. They keep me out of trouble. I work from home, mostly, with the occasional trip out."

"Very good," Jon replied, supposing that explained her mode of dress.

"So, how can I help you?" she asked, finally joining them at the table with her own mug.

"We'd like to ask you about one of your tenants, a Mr Reid. Duncan Reid."

"Oh, yes. He's not a tenant anymore, though. More's the pity."

"We understand he stopped renting from you a few weeks ago, right?"

"That's right, yes. We were sorry to see him go, actually."

"Why's that?" Kate asked.

"Because he was a good tenant. Always paid on time, looked after the place, and he was just a nice man. Unlike the man who came after him. Ugh, he just skipped out on me, disappeared. Left the place in a right mess."

"Duncan Reid rented from you for about ten, eleven months, right?" Jon said, wanting to keep on track and not get derailed by talking about another tenant.

"That's right."

"Did you know he already owned a house?" Jon asked.

"Yes. I did. He told me that he wanted somewhere closer to Redhill that he could use after a night out here. I mean, I thought it was a little curious, but I know other landlords who've had similar tenants who have houses and rent out small flats or terrace houses for them to use close to work and such. It was none of my business, though, really. He paid me, looked after it, and was only there occasionally. I have his actual address if you need it."

"No, no. We have it, thanks," Jon replied.

"Oh, okay."

"And what was your impression of Duncan?"

"I, err, I don't know. He seemed nice enough. He was a tenant, not a friend. I didn't really spend much time with him, but he seemed pleasant enough, though. Why, is he not?"

"He's linked to a case we're looking into, and I was just looking for a character assessment from you, really, to see what you thought of him."

Polly shrugged. "Oh, okay. The house is close by if you want to have a look. It's only round the corner. I can take you if you like."

125

Jon glanced at Kate, who shrugged. "Sure, why not," she said.

"Good, good. I don't think it's in too much of a mess," she replied as she got up and started to lead them out of the house. "I mentioned Mark, didn't I? He was the tenant who came in after Duncan left. He was very eager to get in there, and, well..." She sighed and shook her head. "I don't know. I'm probably being silly and reading into things too much, you know?"

"How come?" Kate asked, as they walked along the street.

"Well, he seemed really nice at first. Said he knew Duncan and was keen to stay at the house. I took a cheque and let him move in. He was so friendly, and as Duncan was a good client, I let my guard down and let him move in before depositing the cheque. Then he was asking all these questions about Duncan, and I just thought it a little odd that he'd be so interested in the previous client."

"And his name was Mark?" Kate asked.

"Mark. Mark Cooper."

"Why was he interested in Duncan?" Jon asked.

"I don't know," Polly said. "Maybe you can help me with him, actually. He disappeared several days ago after moving in, and I had this bad feeling, so I took the cheque to the bank, but it bounced." She sighed. "Yes yes, I know. It was bloody stupid of me to do that, but I honestly thought it would be fine, and it was just a few days. I'll never do that again. And he left the place in a mess. Food and rubbish everywhere. I'm so annoyed at him. I've heard this happen to other people before but…"

"You have?" Kate pressed.

"Yeah. I'm in a few Landlord groups online, and we chat, ask for advice, that kind of thing. I've heard of people not paying their rent or trashing places and disappearing overnight. I never thought I'd have it happen to me, though. I'm so annoyed. Can you help me find him? He owes me money."

"Well, it's not really within our remit, but if we do happen across anything, we'll be sure to let you know," Jon replied.

"Thanks. Here we are," Polly said and led them up to a terrace house that was just a few moments away from Polly's house. She unlocked the door.

Walking in, Jon moved into the front room and looked around. It was nothing spectacular, but it was clean and well maintained, and there was no sign of the mess that Polly had talked about.

"This is nice and clean," Jon commented.

"I had the cleaners in," Polly said.

"So, Duncan lived here?" Jon asked, tuning to Polly, who stood in the doorway to the lounge.

"This is the house he rented from me, yes," she answered.

"I see."

"What's in the basement?" Kate called out from the hallway. Jon walked back to see Kate standing beside an open door beneath the staircase.

"Oh, nothing, I don't think," Polly said. "I don't really go down there. It's a bit creepy. Feel free, though, I thought that was locked."

"It was wide open," Kate said.

"Oh, well, I'll make sure to close it once you're done."

Kate looked up at Jon. "I'll check down here."

"Right you are. I'll look around up here," Jon replied, as Kate moved down the stairs. He'd barely stepped into the kitchen at the back of the house when Kate called up to him.

"Jon?"

He took one quick look around and then wandered back into the hallway to find Polly standing at the entrance to the basement, looking curious but unlikely to head down.

"What is it?" Jon called out.

"I might have found something," she said. He couldn't see her from the top of the stairs, so he made his way down the wooden steps into the concrete rectangle room beneath the house. Lit by a single bulb dangling from the ceiling, there was some shelving against one wall and a few bits of scattered debris, but little else. Kate was crouched close to the corner.

"Oh, there you. Jesus, you gave me some Blair Witch vibes there."

Kate smirked. "Damn, I didn't think of that. I should have just stood in the corner. That would have been awesome."

"No, that would have been cruel."

"In your opinion. Come here, look at this."

"What have you found?" Jon asked and walked over. Behind a small box, Kate pointed to a bright pink purse lying in the dirt, in the shadows. It was completely hidden unless you were right on top of it, and it stood out from everything else in here.

"One of these things is not like the others," Kate sang. "One of these things doesn't belong."

"Sesame Street," Jon said brightly.

"Bingo."

He reached into his inside pocket, pulled out a pair of latex gloves and pulled them on before reaching down and lifting the pink leather purse by the corners. "You're right. This is odd. Let's see…" he muttered and pulled open the flap, revealing an ID card behind a small plastic window.

"Helen Cooper," Jon read and looked up at Kate, frowning. "What is her wallet doing in the corner of this basement?"

"Her surname's Cooper? Maybe she's related to Mark in some way?"

"Maybe."

Kate stood up. "I'll grab an evidence bag from the car and ask Polly if she knows anything on the way out."

Jon followed her to the bottom of the stairs but didn't go up.

"Do you know a Helen Cooper?" Kate asked.

"Um, no, sorry," Polly replied.

"Did Mark not mention a sister or daughter or something?" Jon called up as Kate went to get the bag.

"No, Nothing like that. He didn't talk about his family, just Duncan."

"Hmm," Jon answered as he peered at the photo of the girl on the ID. She was young, in her early twenties maybe, and had that typical neutral expression on her face that was on all ID's these days.

"What's that?" Polly called down. "What did you find?"

Jon looked back at the purse and pulled a face. "Hopefully, nothing."

17

Having dropped the purse off in Horsley Station's small forensics lab, Jon walked back into the office, where Kate was already sitting at her desk. He'd sent her ahead while he stopped by the lab in the hope that she could find something on these new bits of evidence.

It was curious. He wondered if whatever was going on with the Coopers had anything at all to do with this case. It seemed linked to Duncan, given Mark's apparent interest in him. But did that have anything at all to do with the bodies in the walls in Newdigate?

It was probably too early to know and would require some investigating, but he didn't like how this case and the number of suspects seemed to keep growing rather than shrinking.

Who was this Mark, and what the hell was he doing following Duncan around and asking after him? Was he just a friend? Or maybe some kind of former lover or a stalker? Or did he perhaps have unfinished business with Duncan? Maybe this was more sinister than he realised.

He shook his head as he walked through the main office of the SIU, cursing his run away thoughts.

"Jon," a voice called out from behind him. He turned to see the Superintendent standing at his office door. Ray beckoned him over and disappeared inside his office.

Aaah, crap, now what? Did he forget to keep Stingray informed about what he was doing? Probably. He needed to be more careful and play by the rules, he thought as he glanced over at Kate. He'd been heading her way to see if she'd found anything.

She looked at him and shrugged, pulling a face that told him she was just as mystified as he was.

Jon bobbed his eyebrows at her and then made for the DSupt's office. He walked in to find Ray pacing back and forth behind his desk, looking concerned.

"Shut the door, please," Ray asked.

"Sir." Jon did as he was told. "What can I do for you?"

"I've just got off the phone with the ACC," he began, and Jon's heart sank. What was the Assistant Chief Constable up to now? But Ray paused, not offering an answer right away. He looked troubled as he rubbed his jaw with his hand.

"I see, sir," Jon replied, as Ray shook his head. "What seems to be the issue?"

"Alright, I'll just say it, even though it sounds a little like madness to me."

"Very well, sir," Jon replied.

"ACC Ward wants to know why one of my officers is bothering the Miller family."

"What?" Jon asked, shocked.

"I know. I... I'm as surprised as you are. I know who the Millers are, and I know of their reputation. They're dodgy, at best, and I have no idea why the ACC would give them the time of day. I don't know, maybe this has come from higher up or something, but..." Ray sighed. "Okay, so, why are you talking to the Millers?"

"Apart from the obvious?" Jon asked, rising an eyebrow.

"Don't get smart. I'm not in the mood, Jon."

He nodded, wondering about the internal conflict that was going through Ray's head right now. He'd been sent here to the SIU by the ACC to bring the unit into line or—and this was only a guess—find a way to shut it down. ACC Ward did not like the SIU and their investigations into the rich and powerful, and installing a puppet Superintendent was, as far as Jon was concerned, his way to make sure the SIU toed the line.

Was Ray beginning to see another side to the Assistant Chief Constable?

"A suspect in our case has links to the Millers," Jon explained. "We don't know where this suspect is, but we hoped his associates might."

"I see. Okay, and you spoke to one of the Millers today?"

"Two, actually. Nathan visited one."

"Right," he said and shook his head. "Well, this is all shades of messed up. Look, all I can say is, tread carefully. I know I'm holding your feet to the fire constantly, but you also need to follow the leads where ever they go. I get that. I want these murders solved too. I've been in the trenches, I know how it goes. Do your job, but Jon, if you want the SIU to be here in a years time, you need to tread more carefully."

Jon hesitated, surprised by the DSupt's candour, and the fact that he seemed more on Jon's side over this than the ACC's. He didn't expect this state of affairs to last, though. "I'll do my best, sir."

"Good. How's it going?"

"Steady," Jon replied. "We have another lead to follow up." He went on to explain their find at Polly Elliot's rented house.

"Okay, keep me up to date," Ray said. "You can go."

"Thank you, sir," Jon replied and left the office, leaving the DSupt sitting in his chair with a lot on his mind.

Walking back to Kate, he pulled up a chair and sat beside her.

"That was quick," she said.

"I know. Looks like the ACC doesn't like us interrogating the Millers."

"The Millers? He's friendly with the Millers?"

Jon shrugged. "I have no idea. It could have come from higher up or something, but it doesn't look good, whatever the case."

"No, it doesn't. Shit."

"Something weirder than that happened, though," Jon began.

"Weirder?"

"Oh yes, get a load of this. Ray was on our side."

"What?"

"I know. He was just as shocked as we are. He knows who the Millers are and seemed shocked by the ACC's interference. He said we should just tread carefully from now on."

Kate nodded. "Damn. That's good to know, though, that he's with us on this, at least."

"Yep. Alright, so have you found anything?"

"I have, actually." She brought up a page on her screen. "So, I started with Helen, given that we found her purse, and it turns out that she was reported missing today by her mother, Rose Cooper."

"Aaah, okay. That's interesting. If we have her purse, I wonder if we have a crime scene too, in that basement?"

Kate shrugged. "No idea. What I can tell you is that the case was given to DC Ellie Mizaki at Mount Browne. It doesn't look like they have much on the case yet, though."

"Maybe we can give Ellie a boost then, with the purse."

"Yep. We should go and see her. She might know something we don't."

"Sounds good. So, what about Mark Cooper?"

"No criminal record. But, it didn't take much for me to link him with Helen. He's her brother."

"Hmm. Okay, so Mark Cooper seems to know Duncan somehow. Duncan rents that house from Polly, and then moves out..." he checked his notes. "...three weeks ago. Mark moves in a short time after that, asking about Duncan. He seems to know a lot about Duncan. But then he suddenly leaves the property without Polly knowing and cancels his cheque. Then we visit, and find Helen's stuff in the basement, as she's just disappeared."

"Right," Kate agreed.

"But their mother only reported Helen missing, not Mark."

"Seems so, yes."

Jon sat back and frowned. "This all links to the bodies somehow, but how?"

"Do you think it's Duncan?"

"Maybe, but how? He wasn't renting the place when Helen goes missing, but Mark was by the sounds of things. Duncan rented the house out, but Corey was in there when the bodies went in. It's as if someone is following Duncan around, killing people."

"Like he's got a dark cloud following him around."

"But who is that dark cloud? Duncan himself? Or Corey, or Evan?"

"Or Mark?" Kate added.

"Yeah, or him. Or all of them perhaps?"

"All of them? Like some kind of conspiracy?"

"Hmm, maybe not."

"It might be, but maybe don't mention that to Nathan. He might get excited."

"And we wouldn't want that," Jon replied. "Hmm. This is all linked, somehow, but I'm not really sure how. Do you think someone's trying to set Duncan up?"

"Make him out to be the killer, you mean?"

"Yeah. I mean, he fell out with Corey, so he doesn't like him. He doesn't get on with Evan, either. Both have a motive to hurt Duncan or set him up."

"And Mark?"

"I don't know. Mark knows him, for sure."

"True. Polly said he seemed really interested in Duncan. Maybe as more than friends, perhaps?"

"Duncan could be gay, I suppose."

"So maybe he had relationships with Corey and Mark?" Kate suggested.

"Makes sense." Jon thought back to the Lockwood case and the hate that riddled that family. "You don't think this could be another homophobic thing, do you?"

"From who?"

"I don't know. Evan, maybe? Maybe he doesn't like that his brother is gay."

Kate shrugged. "He seems quite a manly man. I guess it could be some toxic masculinity."

Jon nodded but couldn't be sure. All this was pure speculation on their part for now. They needed to know more. "Let's see what we can dig up. See if we have any phone numbers for either of them that we can comb through. If they were friendly, there'd likely be some traces of that in messages and stuff."

"I'll pass it along to the team," Kate said.

Jon felt his phone vibrate in his pocket. He pulled it out and glanced at the caller ID but didn't recognise the number that came up. With a grunt, he answered.

"Hello?"

"DCI Jon Pilgrim," said a male voice with a London accent on the other end of the line. "It's good to speak to you again. This is Irving Miller. We met a few months ago."

"I remember you, Irving," he replied, making sure to say the name aloud so Kate knew who was on the phone. She made an "oh" face at him and moved closer to listen in.

"I'm sure you do. You made quite the impression when you visited, you know, with that plucky partner of yours."

Jon didn't like the man's attitude. "What can I do for you today, Mr Miller."

"Aaah, I see. Straight to the point are we. I see how this is going."

"Good," Jon said.

"No need to be so unfriendly, Jon. I'm a big supporter of the Police and commend the great work you do."

"I'm sure you do. I know the ACC is a big fan of yours."

"I've shared a drink with Miles before at the occasional society function. He's a hard-working and dedicated officer. You could learn a lot from him, Jon."

"Could I?" I bet I could, he thought. Like, how to lick the boots of an organised crime boss, maybe?

"Yes indeed. But that's not why I'm calling you Jon. But, I suspect you know why I'm calling."

"Why don't you enlighten me," Jon said, baiting him.

"If you have questions to ask anyone in this family, Jon, you come to me. I don't like you poking your nose into the private affairs of my family."

"Aaah, well, unfortunately for you, that's kind of my job, and I have certain powers granted to me by the state that allow me to do just that. So if I need to ask Brent some questions, I think that's what I'll be doing, Irving."

There was a moment's silence on the line, as if Irving was thinking his words through before he answered. "I see. Well, good luck, Mr Pilgrim."

"*DCI* Pilgrim, Mr Miller," he corrected him.

"Indeed. I'll see you and Kate around, Jon." The link clicked off.

Kate looked up at him as she sat back in her seat. "He was trying to intimidate you."

"Trying being the operative word," Jon replied. "I'm not going to dance to his tune."

She nodded and smile. "Good. So, what now?"

"Let's go see Ellie, and see what she makes of our lead."

18

After signing in, Jon and Kate moved away from the reception desk in the entrance lobby so the next person in line could be seen.

"Have you been here before?" Kate asked.

"I don't think so, no," Jon replied, looking around the lobby of Mount Browne, the Surrey Police Head Quarters. It was modern, with security doors leading into the building and a huge police logo inlaid into the floor.

"I served my early years here as a PC before becoming a detective," Kate said.

"Nice place?"

"Yeah. I enjoyed my time here, anyway, but I was keen to move into detective work as soon as I could."

"And you got transferred to the SIU?"

"It wasn't the SIU back then, it was the Surrey Murder Team, and it was a bigger group of people. I got partnered with Nathan, which was something of a rite of passage as it turned out."

"I think you mentioned that before."

"Yeah, I probably have," Kate said.

"Remind me what happened."

"Nathan had been demoted after a case went wrong, and he let his conspiracy theories get a little out of hand. He stayed on the murder team, but he was shunned by them. When a rookie joined, they partnered them with Nathan to see how they got on."

"I take it you got on well with him," Jon guessed.

"I did. When they tried to move me on, I requested to stay on as his partner. Some of the other team members were idiots about it, but most were fine. I ended up joining the SIU with Nathan, so it didn't turn out too bad."

"True," Jon agreed. "And then you met me, and your life was complete."

Kate pulled a face. "Riiiight."

"DCI Pilgrim, is it?"

Jon turned to see a short woman with black hair looking up at him. She wore a trouser suit with the familiar Police ID around her neck. "Yes, hi," he said. "And this is DS O'Connell. We're from Horsley Station."

"Nice to meet you. I'm DC Mizaki. How can I help you?"

"Well, it's more to do with us helping you."

"Oh?"

"Yeah, you took on a case today. A missing person's case?"

"Helen Cooper, yes."

"Well, we have some information for you."

"Okay, well, why don't you come with me. We shouldn't discuss this here."

"Of course," Jon said, and with a smile, DC Mizaki led them through the security door and along a corridor to a side room with some sofas and a coffee machine.

"Drink?"

"Sure, thank you," Jon answered.

"Yes, thanks," Kate said.

Ellie busied herself with the drinks. "So, you're on the, um, the Special Investigations Unit at Horsley, right?"

"That's right," Kate said.

"Aren't you linked with the National Crime Agency?"

"That's right. We're still part of the Surrey Police, but we have strong links to the NCA for resources and such."

"Must be good, knowing you have that backup and freedom."

"It can be helpful," Kate agreed.

"I've never been to Horsley Station, is it nice?"

"I like it," Kate said. "I used to work here, back when I was a PC, and if I'm honest, I prefer Horsley. It feels more purpose-built. You'll have to pop over some time, and I'll give you the guided tour."

"I'd like that, thanks," Ellie said.

"Have you been a Detective long?" Jon asked.

"No, I only graduated earlier this year."

"How are you finding it?"

"Yeah, it's good. I like it. I prefer it to the work I was doing before," she said and brought them their drinks. Jon took a sip, pleased to note the coffee was just as terrible here as it had been back up in Nottingham.

"So, what do you have for me?"

"Can you tell us what you know so far about Helen?"

"Sure," Ellie said. "Her mother, Rose, came in earlier to report her as missing. She's not seen her for a few days, and her phone's off, which is very unlike her, apparently."

"Does she live at home with her parents?"

"That's right," Ellie replied. "Mrs Cooper had no idea where she could be. She was quite panicked."

"What about her dad? Does she have any siblings?"

"Her dad is Robert, and her brother is Mark. They didn't come in, though, just her mother. I thought that was a bit odd and she didn't seem to like talking about it."

"Right, that's interesting," Jon replied.

"Why?" Ellie asked.

"Well," Jon said and pulled out the purse, which was sealed inside a clear plastic bag. He handed it to Ellie. "We found that at a house on the outskirts of Redhill. It's Helen's purse. You can see her ID on the inside flap there."

"Oh, wow, yes, that's her. And you found this at a house in Redhill?"

"On the outskirts, but yes. The house had been briefly rented by her brother, Mark Cooper, but he's disappeared somewhere, around or just before Helen went missing."

"Hmm, that is interesting. Why were you investigating Mark?"

"We weren't, not directly, anyway. We have a house in Newdigate where several bodies have been found inside a wall, and our investigation led to the house in Redhill, where we found that in the basement."

"The basement? Okay. Has this been through Forensics?"

Jon nodded and handed over a printed report. "Helen's prints were found, a couple of her hairs too. That's all, though."

"So, how did you end up at this house in Redhill?"

"Via a somewhat convoluted path. The house with the bodies used to belong to a man called Duncan. He rented it out, sold it, and then briefly became a tenant at the house in Redhill."

"Okay. Do you think Helen is involved in these killings? Should I turn this missing person's case over to you?"

"No, you won't do that," said a voice.

Jon looked up to see a man stood at the door, frowning as he looked in at them.

"This is your case, Ellie, and it needs to stay that way."

"But, sir. If Helen is linked to these bodies..."

"No."

Jon stood up. "Hi. I'm DCI Pilgrim from—"

"I know who you are," the man said without looking at Jon. "So this is who you ended up working with, is it Kate?"

"Afternoon, DS Taylor," Kate said, her voice deadpan. She didn't look pleased to see him, and they clearly knew one another.

"It's DI Taylor now," he replied. "I heard you got a promotion too."

Kate shrugged. "That's right, 'Tommy', I did."

"Well done," he said, but he didn't sound impressed to Jon's ears. "So you finally pulled yourself out of the shadow of Halliwell, did you?"

"He's a valuable member of the team, actually," Jon said.

"He's a nut," Tommy said, giving Jon the eye. "I wondered how long it would take for you to show up here and throw your weight around. You're not in the wilds of the north anymore, Jon Pilgrim."

"We're not throwing our weight around," Jon said in protest.

"I beg to differ. You're interfering with the investigation of one of my officers. That's interfering in my book. I'm not having you come here and take the case away from her just because you're all la-di-dah and working with the NCA now."

"That's got nothing to do with this," Kate said.

"I offered it to them," Ellie said. "They didn't come to take it."

"Don't be naive, Mizaki. You'll learn how these things work soon enough. These guys coming down here, from their ivory tower, as if they're gods-gift or something, it stinks. So no, you're not going to take this case away from Mizaki. She's going to work it herself, and I don't want to hear any more about it," Tommy said as he walked to the door. He stopped as he got there and looked back. "It's such a shame, Kate. You had promise. You were good at your job, and you've chosen to follow Nathan into crazy town." He sighed. "See you around, Irish."

Jon watched him walk out, feeling a little shocked by his diatribe against them. He turned and looked at Kate. "Friend of yours? He seems like such a nice man."

"He was on the murder team with us," Kate explained. "He was always a dick, though."

"I've heard stories," Ellie said. "From his point of view, of course."

"I bet. I'm sure he makes himself out to be the righteous one, and turns Nathan into some kind of dangerous psycho."

"Yeah, something like that. It's fairly obvious he's over-inflating himself, though. He does it all the time and thinks we don't notice."

"And he's your boss, right?" Jon asked.

Ellie shrugged a shoulder. "Yeah. He's alright... in small doses."

"Small doses? I think I've had enough of him already. I hope we've not caused you any problems by coming to see you."

"Nothing I can't handle," Ellie replied with a smile.

"Good."

"Why don't you go and talk to Helen's parents," Ellie suggested. "They might be able to help you, shed some light on things."

"Good idea," Jon replied, deciding he liked Ellie. She seemed whip-smart and keen to help. They needed more officers like her. "I think we'll do that first thing tomorrow."

"In that case, why don't I go with you? I'll bring the purse to show them."

"I don't want to cause you any problems with DI Taylor," Jon said.

"You won't. I'll make sure to arrange it in such a way, so he doesn't suspect anything. It'll be fine, you'll see. Here, this is my number," she said, handing Jon a card with her details on it.

Jon did the same. "Thank you, Ellie."

"No problem. I'd better get back to it, anyway. I'll show you out."

"Thanks." Jon followed her through the building with Kate beside him, looking thoughtful after her encounter with Tommy. They said goodbye to Ellie and walked out, making for the car.

"Was that a bit of a blast from the past?" Jon asked.

"Yeah. He was always the joker, and he never liked Nathan. I've often wondered what happened to the guys who used to work at Horsley with us. At least I know where one of them is now. He might be a dick, but I'm glad he's still working."

"Even when they treat you like that?"

Kate shrugged. "He's not my boss, and he was a good detective."

"No, he's not your boss. Hopefully, he won't cause too many problems."

"Just pull rank on him," Kate said.

"Aye, I might."

"Want a helping hand at the house tonight?" Kate asked, looking up at the early evening sky and then back at Jon.

"Sure, why not."

19

Everything hurt. Her wrists hurt, her stomach was twisted into knots that were causing agonising cramps, and her head was swimming.

Helen had no idea what time of day it might be or anything. There were moments when she could have sworn she wasn't even here, entombed in this wall. She was somewhere else, somewhere warm and soft and...

But no, she wasn't.

There was no denying the truth of it, not anymore. As her tummy growled and twisted into another painful cramp, she knew this would be the end for her. She was going to die here, sealed up in this wall. It felt like her own stomach was either trying to eat her from the inside or just gnaw its way out of her altogether.

She found it difficult to focus on anything for too long. Her head pounded and ached as if a hammer kept smashing against the side of her skull, and her mouth felt so dry. She had no saliva at all and hadn't really been able to swallow for who knew how long.

In her moments of lucidity, she knew she'd been hallucinating. She imagined herself in faraway places, free from this nightmare, and living her life, or being hugged by her mother or brother, and being told that everything was okay.

She thought she'd heard people at one point; people moving around and talking close by. But she couldn't be sure.

Had she called out? Had she shouted and tried to get their attention?

She didn't know. Her memories were hazy, and she wasn't even sure if what she'd heard was even real.

Had she missed her chance? Was that it, her one hope of being found, gone?

As the realisation hit her, she screamed. The ragged wail made her throat hurt even more than it already did, and in a fit of rage, she slammed her head against the wall once, twice, three times, before unconsciousness reared its head, as if summoned by her yell and pain.

It rushed up and wrapped her in its pitch velvet cloak, making the world slip away again.

She tried to hang on to reality, to keep from falling into her dreams again, but her desperate clawing for some kind of clarity did nothing to help her, and as the seconds passed, she fell once more into fitful visions.

20

"This is nice, don't you think?" Jon asked as he walked out of the house with Kate the following morning. She'd stayed the night, and it felt kind of right that she was here, with him, like a proper couple, living together.

He liked it.

Part of him wanted to ask her to move in right there and then, but he resisted. And as he thought about it again, he realised it was probably a little too quick for him as well.

He wasn't even all moved in yet, although he wasn't far off being done now. Having Kate help last night had really pushed him on. The place was starting to look a little more like home now, and he was looking forward to kitting it out with all the stuff he needed.

He still didn't have an oven or washing machine yet, though. He'd need to get onto that, but it was tough to do when working such long hours.

"Yeah, it was." Kate gave him a quick peck on the cheek. "Thanks for letting me stay."

"That's okay."

"I'm glad I thought to bring a change of clothes."

"Maybe you should keep some here, you know, just in case?"

"Why, Jon, it's almost as if you're asking me to move in," she said in a mock gasp.

He smiled. "Mmm."

Kate blinked at him. "What was that?"

"Nothing. Just... All in due course."

She pulled a face. "I'm messing with you, Jon. I'd say no if you asked me to move in today. That's a little *too* quick for me, and I think it's a bit quick for you, too."

He nodded in agreement, letting her think she was right. As they walked to the street, he glanced up and down it, wondering if he might see Ariadne or that man again. But, as far as he could tell, there was nothing. He was glad that she hadn't turned up last night, as that might have been a little awkward.

She never did seem to appear whenever Kate was around, so maybe Ariadne was purposely avoiding her.

But, if that was the case, how did she know? Was she watching him somehow? He'd seen enough spy documentaries to know he should be scared and rightfully paranoid if she was taking a keen interest in him. Ariadne was a capable woman, and setting up some ways for her to keep tabs on him would be well within her means and skill set.

With a shudder, he returned his attention to the day, joined Kate in his car, and set off through Guildford. They had a meeting to get to before they headed to the station. He was curious to see how this would play out and if it was in any way related to their case.

Kate directed them to the Cooper household, and as they approached, Jon spotted Ellie standing by her car waiting for them.

"She's keen," Jon remarked.

"She is. I have a feeling she's going to make a good officer."

"Is that your woman's intuition talking?"

"It's a superpower that all women have, Jon. Didn't you know? It's Womb power!"

"Of course… makes perfect sense," Jon said with a raised eyebrow.

"You should see what happens when a bunch of women live together, and we 'synchronise'," she said, giving him a look. "We become invincible."

"That sounds horrifying."

"For men."

Jon laughed. "Alright then, come on, my little superhero, let's see what your super senses make of the Coopers."

"Morning," Jon said, getting out of the car.

"Good morning." Ellie smiled and gestured to two takeaway cups of steaming hot coffee on the roof of her car. "Two Lattes. I didn't know what you'd like so…"

"Aw, thanks," Kate said, grabbing one and taking a sip before turning to Jon. "Can we keep her? Please? I'll look after her."

"If she brings me coffee every morning, I'm all for it," he replied. "Thank you, DC Mizaki."

"Just Ellie, please."

"So, I take it everything went okay, arranging this?"

"Yes. Taylor has no idea you're here. He might suspect something, but not because of anything I did."

Jon nodded. It was as good as he could expect. "Thank you. Are the Coopers expecting us?"

She nodded. "They are. They're primed and ready. I said we'd be there for half eight, so we've got a couple of minutes to kill."

"Just enough time to finish my coffee."

"Where's your accent from?" Ellie asked.

"Aah, you noticed, did you?" Jon asked.

"Hard not to."

"I know, right?" Kate agreed. "Stands out like a sore thumb, doesn't he?"

"I like it. It's, um… earthy."

"Earthy?" Kate said, eyebrows raised.

"Thank you," Jon said, turning to Kate. "You see, someone appreciates my dulcet tones."

"I love you despite them, not because of them."

155

"Shut it, Irish."

Kate stuck her tongue out.

"Promises, promises."

Kate rolled her eyes. "Men! One-track mind."

Ellie chuckled.

"To answer your question, I'm from Nottingham," Jon said, finally.

"Aaah. Robin Hood country," Ellie said.

"That's it."

"I've never been."

"Count your lucky stars," Kate teased, giving her a nudge with her elbow.

"I'm sure it's not that bad," Ellie said.

"No," Jon said. "Kate's right. It can be a little rough in the city sometimes. No different to London, though, I suppose, but that's just cities."

Ellie laughed. "As opposed to rural Surrey, where no one is ever murdered... Um, oh, wait... no. That's not right."

Jon smiled as he finished his coffee, and Ellie took the cardboard cup. "Right then. Shall we?"

Ellie led them up towards the house.

"What was your impression of Rose when you met her?" Jon asked.

"She seemed nice enough. She's a housewife, and he's retired according to what she told me. She seems fairly traditional in her views."

"Okay," Jon replied, as they approached the front door and Ellie pressed the doorbell. Moments later, a woman in her sixties answered it.

"Aah, good morning, detective. Right on time, I see. Please, come in."

"Thank you, Rose. These are my colleagues, DCI Jon Pilgrim, and DS Kate O'Connell."

"Nice to meet you," Rose said, shaking their hands as she smiled at them. "Please, come through."

They were led through to a sitting room, where a man of similar age to Rose waited. He stood and shook Ellie's hand, introducing himself as Robert, then moved on to shake both Kate's and his hands before they settled into the seats.

"Thanks for meeting with me," Ellie began.

"So, you have some news for us?" Rose asked.

"A little, yes," Ellie said. "But I'd just like to ask if you've heard from Helen at all first?"

"Why would we have heard anything?" Robert asked.

"Because most people who disappear either contact their loved ones at some point or just turn up."

"We've not heard anything," Rose answered, placing her hand on Robert's knee.

157

"Very well. Okay, well, I have something here that I just want to show you. My colleagues found what we think is Helen's purse. Forensics confirms it has her fingerprints and DNA on it, but I'd just like for you to have a look at it as well."

"Of course."

"Can you remember what it looked like?"

"Yes. It's a pink purse, leather, and it has her ID in it. A driver's licence, I think."

Ellie pulled out the clear plastic bag. She handed it to Rose. "Don't open the bag, please, but if you can just confirm that this is indeed your daughters."

Rose sniffed as she looked at the wallet, tears twinkling in her eyes. "Yes, this is hers. Where did you find it?"

"I can't be too precise, but it was in a house in Redhill."

"Redhill?" Robert asked. "Why Redhill?"

"That's what we'd like to know," Ellie said. "Did she have any links to Redhill?"

"No," Robert said, sounding offended. "We have no links to that dump."

Jon raised his eyebrows at the comment. It was true that Redhill had an image as being one of the less affluent areas, but he wasn't sure how true that was in real life. He'd not been down here long enough to know for sure.

"Mark..." Rose whispered, almost to herself.

"Sorry?" Ellie said.

"Did you say, Mark?" Jon asked.

Rose nodded.

"He's got nothing to do with this," Robert snapped.

"How do you know?" Rose asked him.

"Because I know."

"Is that your son? Mark?" Jon asked.

"That's right," Rose replied.

"If you say so," Robert muttered, rolling his eyes and sighing.

"Why did he come to mind?" Jon asked, letting Robert's comment go.

"Because that's where he was, last," Rose replied.

"You can't know that," Robert snapped. "You have no idea where he is. He could be anywhere. But we're talking about Rose, not Mark."

"Oh shush," Rose snapped back, before turning to Jon with another smile. "When I last spoke to Mark, he said he was in Redhill, looking for a friend."

"Lord have mercy on my soul," Robert said.

"Um, sorry," Jon said, "but, I just need to ask, is Mark missing too?"

"No," Robert said, a little too quickly.

"Not... really," Rose said. "He moved out not too long ago. We don't see quite as much of him."

Robert grunted.

Jon frowned, sensing something was going on here. Something wasn't quite right with regard to Mark. "Was Helen looking for Mark?"

"I told her not to," Robert said. "He's made his choices in life."

"Choices?" Jon pressed.

Rose sighed, looking thoroughly exasperated by the whole thing.

"That's right. It's his life, and if he chooses to squander the divine gift of life that he's been given and turn to the Adversary, that's on him. But I will not turn from the path of the righteous."

"He came out as gay a little while ago," Rose explained, sounding tired.

"And you don't approve," Jon said, making the logical leap.

"God loves all," Robert said, "but I cannot condone his life choices."

"I've... I've struggled with it, but..."

"You know the Bible's position on this, Rose, it's clear—"

"I know!" Rose snapped, cutting him off. "But he's my son, and I love him. Helen loves him, and you do too. I know you do."

Robert grimaced and took a deep breath. "I... can't... It's against—"

"Oh, do be quiet. Our daughter is missing, Robert. Just get off your high horse for one moment. I don't care what you think the Bible says. God loves Mark just as much as he loves you or me. I know it. He wouldn't want families to split over things like this. It's ridiculous."

"You don't understand—"

"No, you don't!"

"I'm sorry to interrupt," Jon said, "but if we can try to stay focused on the case of your missing daughter, and where your son might be? This links back to a case we're investigating, a murder case, and we need to know if and how this is linked."

"Murder?" Rose asked, shocked.

"Yes. Now, you said you knew he was in Redhill, right?"

"He said so the last time I spoke to him on the phone. But that was a few weeks ago. I've not heard from him since."

"And is that typical?"

"It wasn't until he moved out. Then it became more normal," Rose replied.

"And you said he went there looking for a friend?"

"Yes, Duncan, I think."

"I see," Jon said, the links forming in his head. "Was Duncan a friend, or a lover?"

Robert grunted, but said nothing.

"I... I don't know," Rose admitted.

"And, Helen went looking for him?" Kate asked.

"She did. She knew the last place he'd been was Redhill. She might have spoken to him more than I did, actually. She might have known where he lived."

Jon nodded, certain that she did know where Mark had been living. But, did she know her brother as well as she thought she did? Had he taken her? But then, what was the link to Duncan?

"And, you have no idea where Mark might be?"

"No... although, I think I might know one person who might."

"Oh, really?" Ellie said.

"Yes," Rose replied. "Sorry, detective. I followed your advice and went looking for clues after our interview yesterday, to see if there was anything that might help either of them."

"And you found something?"

"I think maybe, yes. I remembered one of Mark's close friends was a girl called Skye Simpson. I think if anyone might know where he is, she might."

"And what about friends of Helen?"

"I've already called around them all. I know them better than Mark's friends. But no, no one seems to know anything."

"Can you give me their details?" Ellie asked.

"Of course, I made a list. Look, here," she said, and handed a sheet of paper to Ellie.

"Thank you, Mrs Cooper. I wish you'd given me these earlier."

"I know, I'm sorry."

Jon turned the conversation to Mark again and asked if they knew Evan Reid or Corey Grant, but Rose didn't recognise any of the names he mentioned. But it soon became clear they were at the limits of the Coopers usefulness. Plus, Robert was being singularly unhelpful.

"Was that useful?" Ellie asked as they walked back to their cars.

"I think so," Jon replied.

"Certainly," Kate added. "Thank you for arranging this for us."

"My pleasure. Seriously. And, if I can help further, let me know."

"We will," Kate agreed.

"So, what will you be doing next?" Ellie asked.

"Heading back to the station and seeing where we are with our investigations," Jon said. "I think you should get Forensics onto that house in Redhill, by the way."

Ellie smiled. "Way ahead of you. They're probably already there by now."

"Good job."

21

"I hate family drama like that," Jon said as they made their way back into Horsley Station. "It always causes way too much pain and heartache."

"And murders," Kate added.

"That's what I was referring to," Jon replied with a smile on his face. "My pain and heartache at having to deal with the paperwork."

"Very droll. So, I take it we'll be going to visit this Skye Simpson?"

"I think so. I have no idea if Mark is linked to these bodies in the walls, but providing we don't have any further big leads to chase up, we need to tie up these loose threads and see where they take us."

"Hmm."

"Pilgrim!" It was the Superintendent, standing at his door with a face like thunder. "Get in here, now!"

"Sir," Jon replied, and gave Kate a glance.

She shrugged, apparently as mystified as he was about why the Super would be so angry at him. "I think you'd better go and see what's up," she said.

"Yeah, I think so," he said. He went to walk to the office door and then turned back to her. "If I should die, see that my body is used for science."

"You're not going to die," Kate stated.

"How do you know? He looked about ready to gnaw my limbs off. This could be the end for me. Maybe start thinking about what you'd write on my gravestone."

"Here lies Jon Pilgrim, he made tea the wrong way."

"You spelt 'right' wrong."

"Pilgrim!" It was Ray again.

"Ooops," he said and set off for the office, leaving Kate behind. He was making light of the situation, but Stingray was clearly annoyed about something, so Jon made sure to take a breath and remove the smile from his face as he walked into the office, shutting the door behind him.

"What the hell are you up to, hmm? Why have I got DCI Malcolm Dean calling me up from Mount Browne, asking why the hell you're interfering with a case over there?"

Aaah, Jon thought. He hadn't actually thought that DI Taylor would pass the issue up the chain of command, but clearly, he'd underestimated how much the man thought of himself.

Jon took a breath and collected his thoughts before answering. "We were not trying to interfere with any investigation, sir. We were following a lead we found at one

165

of the properties we were looking at, and it led to a missing person's case over at Mount Browne. We spoke with the officer who had taken the case, and her superior took offence to that."

Ray sighed as he listened, staring at Jon with his dark eyes. "This is two complaints about your conduct on this case in as many days, Jon. This doesn't look good. You're putting me in a very difficult position. If the ACC gets wind of this..." he sighed.

"I'm sorry, sir, but I don't believe I was doing anything wrong. The Millers are legitimate suspects, and we were not trying to cause problems at Mount Browne. DI Taylor clearly hates Kate and Nathan, and by extension, me and the SIU as a whole. He used to work with Kate on the murder team. That's all it is."

"I'm aware of his history, and his poor reputation is well known." He let out a long breath. "Watch what you're doing, Jon. Tread carefully."

Was that sympathy from the Superintendent? "Are you starting to like it here, sir?"

Ray raised an eyebrow and glared at him.

"It's okay if you do," Jon pressed, trying on a hint of a smile to see how it went over.

"Shut that smart mouth of yours, Pilgrim," Ray snapped. "It's no wonder you rub people up the wrong way."

"I've not been rubbing anyone in the office yet, sir."

"Get out and solve this case. I'll have less of your cheek, too."

"Sorry, sir," Jon apologised and walked out as Ray collapsed back into his chair.

Jon strode across the office, making for Kate, who was standing with Nathan.

"Fox," Jon said as he drew close, calling him by his nickname.

"Loxley," Nathan said in greeting, using the nickname Nathan had coined for him.

"What have you got for me?"

"We've got the identities of some of the bodies we found in the wall at the Woods' house. I won't go into details, but they're all either runaways or disenfranchised people who didn't have many people looking out for them. People who wouldn't be missed, in other words. A couple were homeless, most were out of work. They'd already slipped through the cracks when the killer found them."

"They were targeted then," Jon surmised. "The killer was looking for people who wouldn't be missed. He, or she, I suppose, was being clever about this."

"That was my conclusion, too," Nathan replied. "So far as we can tell, none of the victims knew one another, and there was no link between them and either Duncan or Evan. However, one of them did have a link to Corey."

"What kind of link?"

"He was a user, a druggy. He was caught dealing and using several times, and seemed to know members of the Miller family. I don't know if he knew Corey directly, but it's certainly possible."

"Shit. We need to find Corey," Jon said. "Any luck on that front?"

"No, nothing," Nathan replied.

"Damn. Alright then," he looked over at Kate, "Skye Simpson it is then."

22

"Well, I'm sure this is going to go down like a lead balloon," Jon said as they pulled up outside the Leatherhead primary school that Skye worked at.

"Yeah, I'll bet the head will want a word with Skye after we pay her a visit."

"Aye. Nothing for it, though. I'm not waiting. Come on." Jon led the way in, following the signs for the reception as he thought about the case and the merry chase it had led them on. No sooner had they found one clue, before another popped up, leading them further and further away from the bodies in the wall.

At this rate, he was beginning to doubt they'd ever actually find out who killed them. For all they knew, it was someone they hadn't even met yet. Someone who'd snuck into the house while Corey was renovating it and proceeded to seal up the bodies in the wall without either Corey or anyone else knowing.

This was a messed up and messy case, and he was starting to hate it, not least because it was getting him into trouble with the top brass.

Jon sighed as he walked and wondered if he was being a little more reckless than usual? But if he was, what was causing it? Ariadne, maybe? Or the threats from the stranger? He'd not seen them for over a day now, and he was starting to wonder if maybe that was it. Would they show up again? Would Ariadne grace his doorstep, or would the man follow through on his threats?

He wasn't sleeping well; he knew that much. Was he stressed? Maybe.

Having Kate over last night had settled him a little better than previous nights, but he still found himself waking up in the middle of the night, disturbed by some tiny noise that was probably the house settling or the pipes expanding or something.

Jumping at shadows wasn't what he usually did, but something about recent events had put him on edge. He didn't have the luxury to think about it too much right now, though. He had a job to do and a killer to find.

"Good morning," Jon said to the receptionist in the entrance hallway.

"Morning, how can I help you?"

He held up his warrant card. "We're looking for Miss Simpson. We'd like to speak to her."

"Oh, really? Okay, um, erm... She'll be teaching. I'll need to find someone who can take over for her. Can you bear with me for a moment, please?"

Jon nodded and stepped away from the desk. He looked over at Kate. "Lead balloon."

"Yup," she agreed, as they waited. The receptionist spoke to a couple of people on the phone before someone appeared and introduced themselves as Mrs Carr, the headteacher, before leading them through the school. The corridors were filled with the sounds of young children playing, talking and shouting as they went about their lessons.

It was the sound of innocence, and it made Jon smile to hear it, but also gave him a heavy heart when he thought about the terrible people that were out there, just beyond those gates.

"Is she in trouble?" the head asked as she led them through the hallways.

"No," Kate replied. "We just want to ask her a few questions. She might know something that could be useful in a case. That's all."

"Oh, okay. That's good."

Jon pressed his lips together and read between the lines of the head's question. She wanted to know if Miss Simpson was a danger to the young children she was teaching and if they needed to send her home.

"We'd tell you if we thought there was anything you should be worried about," Jon added.

The headteacher smiled and looked a little embarrassed as she realised the true nature of her question had been rumbled. "She's in here. If you'd just like to wait out here?"

"Of course," Jon said, and stood back while the head popped in and summoned Skye out of the classroom. She walked out, handing the class over to a teaching assistant. Her expression was one of curiosity as she eyed them.

"Is everything okay? Can I help you?" Skye's gaze tick-toked back and forth between them and the head.

"These people want to speak with you privately. I think classroom 3b is free, if you want to take them there."

"Oh," Skye said, as Jon showed her his warrant card.

"We won't be long, Miss Simpson. We just have a few questions for you."

"Um, okay, sure."

"I'll take over your class," Mrs Carr said, and then touched Skye on the arm. "If you need some time, it's okay. We can cover you."

"Thanks, but um, I'm sure I'll be fine." She looked nervous as she waved them up the corridor. "It's this way."

"Should I be worried," Skye asked.

Jon pulled a face. "Do you have anything you think you need to worry about?"

"Um, no. I don't think so."

"Then probably not."

"Okay," Skye said, and led them into an empty classroom and closed the door behind them. "How can I help you?"

"Thanks for seeing us," Jon said, and introduced himself and Kate to her. "We just have a few questions for you related to the case we're working on and hoped you might be able to help us out."

"I'll try," she replied.

"Good, thank you. Let's dive right in, shall we? Do you know Mark Cooper?"

She frowned. "What's this about?"

Interesting, Jon thought. Rather than just say yes or no, she seemed to get immediately suspicious. He wondered why. "We're a little concerned and think he might have got himself caught up with something. Do you know him?"

She took a moment to answer but seemed to come to a conclusion about whatever she was going to say, and took a deep breath. "Yes, I know him. We've been friends for years. Why?"

"His parents are a little worried about him."

"Really?" she scoffed at Jon's statement. "I'd be shocked if they were. They hate him."

"Hate him?"

"Yeah. Just because he's gay. It's bloody ridiculous. His dad's the worst. He's some kind of fundamentalist freak. It's sick. How they can throw out and disown their own child like

173

that is disgusting, and you come here saying they're worried about him? I doubt that very much."

"His mother expressed concern," Kate said.

She grunted. "Did she?" Sky sighed. "Well, okay, she might be a little worried, I suppose. She's tried to keep in touch as much as she can, I think, but his dad rules that house, not her, and he'd never have Mark back."

"So you know a bit about the family dynamic, then?" Jon asked.

"Mark's talked about it a few times, yeah. They have no idea what it's done to him. It broke him when they threw him out."

"I bet," Kate sympathised. "So, did he come to you?"

"He's relied on several friends over the last year or so, sleeping on their sofas and stuff."

"On yours?"

"Occasionally," Skye replied, her face neutral. She was still suspicious.

"What can you tell me about Duncan?" Jon asked.

"Duncan? Heh, well, you have done your research. Yeah, he's dated Duncan on and off over the last year. I think Mark wanted something more serious, but he got a little obsessed with Duncan, and he seems to have backed off. The whole thing has been an off-and-on-again roller coaster."

"Obsessed?" Jon asked, curious.

"Yeah. Mark would talk about him all the time, just constantly referring back to him. Saying Duncan wouldn't do that, or Duncan likes this, you know? He was smitten."

"But Duncan didn't return these feelings?" Kate asked.

"I've never really met the man, but he didn't seem quite as interested in Mark."

"So Mark was obsessed with him, would you say?" Jon said.

"I think that's probably true, yeah. I think he's just stringing him along and using Mark whenever he feels like it. I've told Mark this, but... well, I think it might be starting to sink in a bit."

"What about Helen? Do you know her?"

"I've met her a few times, yeah. She's nice. She never judged Mark for who he was, she always just accepted him, and she kept in touch, too."

"And do you know where she is now?"

"No, sorry. Why?"

"Her mother reported her missing." Jon watched Skye's expression change to one of shock.

"Oh, really? She's gone? You're sure?" The change in her demeanour was stark. She'd gone from suspicious and disinterested to shocked and concerned very quickly, which spoke volumes about how out of character this was for Helen.

"As far as we can tell. We're trying to find her, and we were hoping that Mark might know something."

"Well, I guess he might. I'm sorry, I didn't know she was missing." She looked a little upset actually, Jon thought.

"She's not answering her phone, apparently, which is unlike her, according to Mrs Cooper," Kate said.

"Yeah, that is unlike her. She always answered the phone to Mark."

"So, do you know where he is?" Jon pressed, keen to get an answer on this quickly.

Skye sighed. "I do, yes. He's at mine."

"Yours?"

"He's been sleeping on my sofa for a few days. Do you want me to take you to him?"

23

Driving across town and out towards Ashtead, Jon glanced into the rear-view mirror. Skye sat in the back, her elbow on the window ledge as she gazed out at the passing houses and greenery.

Given her initial confrontational attitude, he wasn't sure that she would have admitted to Mark being at her place if he hadn't mentioned that Helen was missing.

She was clearly protective of him, but that wasn't very surprising, given his history with his family. He had to rely on his friends so much more than everyone else, and Skye was obviously a good friend.

"You're protective of him, aren't you," Jon said.

Skye turned and met his gaze in the mirror. She shrugged. "Yeah, I guess. He's not got many people looking out for him, so..."

"You're a good friend."

"Hmm," she said, turning away. She was still keeping them at arm's length. "It's up here. Turn left." She directed them through the village before they eventually pulled up at her house.

Jon shared a brief glance with Kate before they got out and followed Skye up her garden path to the dark bricked semi on a quiet side street off one of the main roads through the village. He hoped that this particular lead would either come to a close with this visit or actually lead them somewhere constructive. The last thing he wanted was to get in here and find that Mark had disappeared again.

However, that fear was soon dispelled when they found Mark sitting in the house watching TV, a crumb covered plate on the table before him. He turned the TV off and stood when Skye walked in, followed by Jon and Kate.

"Glad you're here," Skye said, and gave him a weak smile.

"Hey, what's this all about?"

Jon showed his ID and introduced himself and Kate. "We need to talk to you," Jon said, as they all sat.

"Okay, sure. What about?"

"Well, firstly, did you know your sister's gone missing?"

"What?" Mark said, shocked. Skye sat beside him. She grabbed his hand and put her arm around his back. "When? When did she go missing?"

"A few days ago. Your mother reported it to the Police yesterday."

"Oh my god. Are you sure? I mean, I spoke to her, just the other day." He pulled his phone out. "Let me try her."

"Your mother's already tried that," Jon said.

"Not this number, she hasn't. She's got another phone, just for me," he said and hit dial.

"Another phone?"

He nodded. "Dad looks at her phone. He checks to make sure she's not calling or messaging me. So she's got a pay-as-you-go that I can talk to her on."

"Clever. We'll need that number before we go."

"Sure. It's my old one. I used to have it to hide stuff from him too. It's ringing."

After a moment, Mark ended the call. "It went to the answerphone."

He tried a few more times, but still, she didn't answer.

"Shit," he cursed to himself. "Do you have any idea where she might be?"

"Well, we found her purse in the basement of a house in Redhill. One that you rented for a few days."

"Oh, crap." Mark sighed. "I'm sorry. Yeah, she saw me there, didn't she? Oh shit, what was she doing going back there?"

"She knew you lived there?"

"Yeah, she knew. Crap."

"Why would she go there?" Jon asked. "I mean, apart from it being where you lived."

"Because of Duncan… Well, because of me, because I was trying to get close to him, and I thought that by staying in that house, I might… I don't know. I just wanted to be near to him."

"To Duncan?"

"Yes. He's been so cold with me again recently. I never know where I am with him."

"He's leading you on," Skye said. "I've told you, you need to forget about him. He's no good for you. You'll just end up getting hurt."

"I know. I know. And now it looks like my antics have hurt Helen too."

"She's responsible for her own actions," Skye said.

"But if I hadn't been staying there, it would never have happened. Oh, this is all messed up."

"Can you run us through it?" Kate asked.

Mark sighed. "It's just as I said. I wanted to be close to Duncan because he wasn't taking my calls again. I know he see's other people, I've seen him with a woman recently, but I can't help it. It's like, he's got a hold over me. Anyway, I thought I'd stay in that house. It's where he's lived pretty much the whole time I've known him. I mean, I know he has another place, but I've never seen it. So we just hung out there, in Redhill. It's kind of special to me. So I rented it."

"But only for a few days," Jon said.

"That's my fault," Skye admitted. "I went and saw him, and we had a long talk about what he was doing. I convinced him to come back to mine." She turned to Mark, looking sorry for him. "Duncan is leading you on. He's no good for you."

"I know. I just… it's hard, you know?"

"What about Polly? You didn't pay her. You cancelled the cheque."

"Is that right?" Skye asked.

"Money's tight," Mark protested. "I'll pay her, I will. But I can't pay her right now. I don't have it. I didn't want to cancel the cheque, but… It would bounce anyway if she tried to take the money."

"Oh, Mark," Skye groaned. "You should have said."

"Sorry. Anyway, enough about me. We need to find Helen."

"Any ideas about that?" Kate asked.

"I… I don't know. No. No ideas. But, she must have been in the basement if her purse was found down there."

"That would be my guess, too," Jon said. "It also suggests a struggle."

"Do you think she's hurt?"

"I hope not," Jon replied, as he eyed Mark for a moment. "So, you hung out with Duncan a while, right?"

"Yeah," Mark replied.

"So, what is he like?"

Mark shrugged. "He's… Well, I like him."

Jon nodded as his thoughts turned to the bodies in the walls. He needed to know how this all connected and wondered how to phrase the questions to get to what he

181

wanted out of Mark. "Did he ever talk about the house he inherited from his mother?"

"Oh," Mark replied, looking off into the middle distance. "Um, yeah. He sold it, I think. Yeah, that was right. He rented it out to a guy. Cameron or Cody, was it?"

"Corey," Jon confirmed.

"That's right, yeah. They had a falling out. I think they were dating, actually. Oh yeah, now I remember. He was angry at Corey because he wouldn't tell Duncan what he did for money. He suspected that Corey was into some dodgy stuff, like, criminal stuff, and confronted him about it. They argued and fell out, and then Corey moved out. Duncan sold the place after that."

"That's right, to the Woods family."

"I guess. I don't know if he ever told me who bought it... Heh, yeah, but he did tell me that his brother wanted it but didn't get it."

"You know about Evan, then?"

"Oh yeah. He's a piece of work, alright. A real dipshit."

"Did he not like that you and Duncan were a couple?"

"Oh, no, nothing like that. He wasn't a bigot. He just had issues with Duncan being respectful to their family and the house. I think he had problems in the head too, from the fighting he'd been made to do."

"He suffers from PTSD," Jon confirmed.

182

"That's right. I never liked him. He's got a hell of a temper on him. I felt like I was walking on eggshells whenever I was around him."

"I see."

"So, um, what is this all about? Is it just Helen, because I don't think Duncan had anything to do with her, really."

"It's related to that, but no, Helen isn't the main focus of our case. Someone else is heading up that line of enquiry."

"So, what is it about?"

"I don't really want to say too much right now," Jon said. "But you've been very helpful."

"Sure. So, do you have any idea where Helen is?"

"We're following up some leads," Jon replied, but inside, he knew there were relatively few at this point and wasn't sure how or when they'd find her. "We'll let you know if we hear anything."

Mark sighed before picking up his mobile. "I'll try her again. You never know."

Jon nodded and stood up. "Thank you for your time, Mark."

He smiled at them and then looked suddenly shocked. "Hello?" he said. "Oh, this is Mark Cooper, who's this? Oh, I see. Is Helen there?"

Jon frowned at Mark, wondering what the hell was going on. Who was answering Helen's phone?

"I was just calling because, well, there's a couple of detectives here. Um… hold on." Mark pressed the phone to his chest. "What are your names again?"

"Who are you speaking to?" Jon asked.

"A detective. Mizaki or someone?"

"Give me the phone," Jon snapped, and reached his hand out.

"Oh, um, okay," Mark stammered and handed the phone to him.

"DC Mizaki? Is that you?"

"Jon, hi. You're with Mark Cooper?"

"Yes, where are you?"

"At the house in Redhill. I think you had better get here. There's something I need to show you."

24

"You're sure Ellie didn't say anything else?" Kate asked.

"Nope. She said we should just get there as quick as we could," Jon replied as he sped through traffic, taking the opportunity to pop the lights and siren on. It wasn't often he got to use the concealed lights on the pool car, but this was as good an opportunity as ever. "It sounded like she couldn't really chat over the phone. She ended the call pretty quickly."

Something was up, he knew it. He could hear it in Ellie's voice on the phone. They'd found something, something big, something juicy.

"What do you think it is?" Kate asked, curiosity in her voice. She wanted to know what was going on just as much as he did.

"More bodies in a wall, maybe?" Jon suggested.

"Could be. Ellie wasn't there for the ones at the Woods' house. It would be a pretty major find."

"And it would mean that the case is ours," Jon said, enjoying the idea that this would piss DI Tommy Taylor off something chronic. Yeah, that really was a delicious thought.

"Yeah. Which means Taylor can suck it."

"My thoughts exactly," Jon agreed as he pressed on, making their way towards Redhill. "What did you think to what Mark had to say?"

"Which bit?"

"Any of it. He didn't have much nice to say about Evan, did he?"

"No, not really. I get it though. He's an intimidating man, that's for sure. Scary too. That level of obsession with his old house is a little intense. Makes you wonder what he knows."

"Mmm, I know what you mean," Jon replied. "Do you think he did it?"

"I don't know. I really don't. If I knew that, we wouldn't be out here chasing ghosts."

"I guess not. So, what are you up to tonight?"

"I'm seeing a friend, sorry," Kate replied.

"Harper?"

"Yeah. Going for a drink and a catch-up."

"Great, sounds good. Hmm, I might have to take myself shopping, provided we don't finish too late."

"I did mine the other day. Tesco twenty-four-hour shopping in Leatherhead. Nothing beats wandering around the empty aisles at one in the morning."

"Did you do it in your jammies?"

"Heh, no. I've seen people walking around in their PJs, though. You see some interesting characters that late at night, that's for sure."

"I bet," Jon replied, as they came around the final corner, to find the usual collection of marked and unmarked police vehicles parked up outside Polly's rental property, along with the reams of police tape, cordoning off the area. Jon pulled up and got out.

"Right, let's go and see what Ellie has for us."

"Look, there's Polly," Kate said, pointing to a woman talking to an officer on the cordon.

"So it is," Jon replied, and marched over. Polly stood at the police tape with a worrying frown. It seemed like she was chewing on the inside of her cheek.

"Everything okay, Polly?" Jon asked.

"No. Everything's not okay, detective. They won't let me through or tell me what's going on. I thought it was just a forensics sweep, but then all these other officers turned up, along with that ambulance and fire truck. What the hell are they doing in there?"

Jon raised an eyebrow at the additional emergency vehicles and wondered the same. "I don't know," he admitted. "I was just told to get here."

"Great, so you're in the dark as much as I am. Perfect."

"For now. I'm going to head in and see what's going on, and I promise I will come back and tell you as much as I can. Okay?"

Despite still being unhappy, she seemed to calm down.

"Okay, thank you."

"No problem," he said.

"Sit tight," Kate added as they signed in without issue and started to make their way closer to the house. As they closed in on the front garden, Jon spotted DI Taylor, and their eyes met.

The reaction was instant.

Tommy's expression turned to one of fury, and he strode over. "Oh no. No, no, no. No, you don't. You're not coming in here and taking over. No way."

Jon raised his hands. "We were just told to come," he said.

"By who? I know I don't want you here."

"By DC Mizaki," Jon replied.

"Oh, well then, if a DC said so, then I guess I should just shut my mouth, right? Piss off. No. You're not coming in—"

"What did you find?" Kate asked, cutting him off.

"None of your beeswax, Irish. This one's mine."

"I think it's Ellie's, really," Jon said.

"Don't get smart."

"I'll try not to. I wouldn't want to confuse you."

Tommy's eyes bugged at the comment. He went to say something, but Kate spoke up again.

"Are there bodies in the wall?"

The question brought Tommy up short. He turned to Kate. "What?"

"Bodies? Are there some in the walls?"

"How did you...?"

"We've been investigating a house in Newdigate, where we found eight bodies, bagged up and stuffed in a hollow wall. The case led us to talk to Ellie."

Tommy seemed to tremble with barely restrained rage. His mouth worked as if he was trying to form a sentence but didn't know where to start. "Damn it," he said finally.

"It is, isn't it?" Jon said.

"You still shouldn't be here."

"Do I have to pull rank on you, DI Taylor?" Jon asked.

"I'll be sure to report this, you know."

"Please do, but this is our case. You just happened to stumble onto it. It's no biggy, really. These things happen. Now, if it's okay with you, I think we'll go and have a look."

"Do what the fuck you want," Tommy snapped and stormed off up the garden path and back onto the street.

"Told you it was bodies in the wall," Kate said.

"Yeah, you did. So, what do you want? A gold star?"

"Yes please, and a sticker," Kate replied with a bright smile. They were directed to a nearby tent, where they pulled on some forensics suits before they made their way inside. Work lights had been set up, lighting up the hallway as people moved around, coming and going from the basement. Jon could hear talking and loud voices coming from below. What was going on?

As they neared the stairs leading down, an officer stopped them. "Can I help?"

"DC Mizaki called us in," Jon explained.

"Well, things are a little crowded down there for now. I think you might need to wai—"

"Jon, Kate, good to see you," Ellie said, appearing at the top of the basement stairs. "I thought I heard your voices outside."

"Yeah, had a run in with Inspector Twat," he said quietly.

Ellie smirked. "Come down. I've got something interesting to show you."

"Sure," Jon said, and they followed her down into the basement. They were clustered mainly around the far wall where the freestanding metal shelves had been. But the shelves had been moved, and what Jon saw was bizarre.

"Is that... is that a false wall?"

"It is," Ellie said. "And if you hadn't been to see Mark Cooper when you did, we might never have found it."

"What? What happened?" Kate asked.

"We were doing that sweep of the house I mentioned. The Forensic officers that were down here heard what sounded like a phone ringing, but it was coming from behind that wall."

"Oh, shite."

"So we got everyone down here, and once we started looking, we discovered the false wall and broke through. That's when Mark called again, and we found the phone."

"Just a phone?" Kate asked.

"Hold your horses, I'm getting there," Ellie replied.

Jon gave Kate a look. "That told you, you eager beaver."

"Sure did."

"Once we were in there, we started to hear noises. Banging and a voice behind the next wall. It was a fresh wall, too. The cement had only just dried."

"You mean…" Jon started.

"Someone is behind that wall, and they're alive."

"Oh my god," Kate said.

"Can we have a look?" Jon asked, and Ellie nodded, letting them through. It was a very tight space, and although it was lit up, shadows played across the walls as the team moved. Police officers and firemen were working hard to knock out the bricks and get to the person behind.

They'd made good progress, but there was a wooden partition behind the bricks, keeping the victim hidden from view.

Jon could hear her though. He could make out the soft pleas for help that came from within.

Keen to help, Jon started to muck in with the effort to free whoever was trapped, and Kate did the same. It was simple, drudge work, but they all worked together to get it done.

It seemed to take forever, but after what felt like an age, they could finally get to the wooden partition wall and set to work on freeing that too. The scene that greeted them as they lifted the wood away was like something from a nightmare.

A young woman of about twenty years of age was trussed up behind the wall, sandwiched between bodies in black bags. The girl was alive but in a hell of a state. She simply collapsed into the arms of the officers, firemen and paramedics as they freed her.

Ellie recognised her right away as Helen.

Jon watched in mute horror as the girl was brought out, placed on a bright orange plastic board, and assessed by the paramedics before she was eventually moved. No one really said much as they watched this latest victim of this sick and twisted killer. All Jon wanted was for her to live. She needed to survive, not only because she was a key witness, but to hopefully put a stop to the string of murders that the killer had got away with so far.

A short time later, once the girl was wrapped in blankets and made ready, she was removed from the house to be taken to the closest hospital for treatment.

The mood in the room was sombre, but their work had only just begun, as forensics set to work taking down the rest of the wall and removing the bodies from it.

"Polly's going to see her being taken out," Kate said.

"I think she deserves some kind of explanation. I'll go and talk to her."

This would be a long afternoon.

25

It was late by the time Jon got home. Night had fallen, and he was in something of a mess from all the dust floating around that basement.

They'd found four more bodies in the wall, all of them bagged and in a fairly advanced state of decay and decomposition. They'd been removed from the property reasonably quickly, leaving them with the remains of the hidden space.

It was cleverly done, and behind the shelves, the concealed door into the hidden partition was almost invisible. He almost dare not think what might have happened to Helen if he hadn't been to see Mark and caused him to ring Helen's phone. Would the Forensics team have found the hidden door? Would they have freed Helen in time to save her? These were disturbing questions, but they were probably not worth worrying about. They had found the girl. She was alive and safe in the hands of the NHS, and that was all that mattered as far as he was concerned.

But even with this discovery, until they found out if Helen knew anything, until she told them what she knew, they were still no closer to catching this killer. But they'd have to wait.

Helen was dehydrated, starving and delirious. She'd be no use to them until she was feeling better.

He had his suspicions regarding the case, but that's all they were, with no solid evidence to back up anything.

Jon sat in his car and leant back, closing his eyes as he tried to relax. He was tired. Helping free Helen from the wall had been hard, back-breaking work, and he was paying for it now. All he wanted to do was to get inside, have something to eat, and get to bed. His planned trip to the shops would have to wait until tomorrow, or whenever it was that he finally got some time to himself.

Right now, he felt like just ordering a pizza or something and being done with it.

With a grunt and a supreme effort of will, he opened the door to the car and got out, making for the house. At the gate to his tiny front garden, getting a funny feeling, he paused and looked around. The road was lined with cars and vehicles of all kinds, but he couldn't see anything wrong or out of place. He also couldn't see Ariadne anywhere, which was something of a relief.

He could do without her turning up tonight, he thought as he dismissed his feelings of being watched, and moved to the door, fumbling with his keys before finally opening it.

"Hey, Pilgrim, I've got a message for you."

Jon turned, suddenly alert and tense. A man barrelled into him, tackling him full in the chest and throwing him into the front hallway of his house. He hit the floor with a crunch that took his breath away as he struggled against his attacker. The man sat up, practically on top of him, and tried to reach for him, but Jon fought back, pushing the man's hands and arms away from his neck.

"Get off me," Jon yelled.

"Stop fighting it," the man hissed through his teeth as he tried again and pushed in. Jon's strength was failing him. The man finally got both hands around his neck and squeezed.

"No," Jon gasped as he pulled on the man's arms and hands, trying to pry them off.

"Vassili says 'hi', by the way," the man said as spittle flew from his mouth. "You took his life, now he takes yours. It's only right, yeah?"

"Not today." Jon grunted and brought his knee up into the man's groin. His grip loosened, and he bent closer. Jon threw a keen right hook, born from his desperation to live, and caught him right on the jaw. He let go and fell into the hallway wall.

Jon turned, coughing and gasping, sucking air into his lungs as he crawled away into his front room, away from his attacker. He felt weak and didn't really know where he was going, but anywhere was better than in the hallway at this point.

"Oi, where you going?" the man called out.

Terrified, Jon twisted onto his back in time to see the man get back to his feet and wipe the blood off of his chin. He had a cracked lip from the punch, but didn't seem otherwise incapacitated by it.

"Impressive hit," the man said.

"I have more where that came from," Jon threatened him.

"And I just need to get this done," the man said. He reached for something at the small of his back and pulled out a knife that glinted in the street light that filtered through the open door.

Aaah, shit, Jon thought. He was unarmed and in no state for a knife fight. He could see this going only one way, and he didn't like his odds at all.

"Now, hold up," Jon said. "Let's talk about this. What's Vassili paying you?"

"None of your bloody business."

"I'll double it," Jon said, with no idea if he could actually afford such a thing or not. Not that he had any intention of paying this man, of course.

The man paused, his eyebrows raised.

"Yes, okay. I'll pay you. Please, just, put the knife away."

The man smiled. "Nice try, but if I don't do this, Vassili will find me and make me pay in blood."

"He's in prison," Jon said, desperate to find an angle that worked.

"So what? He knows people, dangerous people who'd kill me if I pulled out."

"But we can work this out."

"No fuckin' way," the man declared, and raised the dagger as he lunged for him.

Glass shattered as something zipped into the room. Blood flew from the man's leg, just above the knee. He dropped and yelled in pain as he clutched his thigh.

Jon could see blood flowing freely over the man's hands as he gripped his wound. "What the hell? Arrgh, what did you do? Ugh. Christ, it hurts."

Stunned, Jon just stared at the man in utter bewilderment. What had just happened to him? This was crazy. If he didn't know better, he'd guess that the man had just been shot. But who would do that? No sooner had he thought about it than the answer hit him like a tonne of bricks.

It was obvious, he thought as he pushed himself up into a sitting position on the floor, his whole body aching from the day's work and the fight.

A moment later, he heard footsteps that sounded all too familiar, and he knew who was coming. Sure enough, the dark-haired beauty, Aridane, stalked into the room wearing a long red and black dress with a generous slit up her right leg, revealing pale flesh.

She smiled at him as she walked in. She was followed by another woman who was the polar opposite of Ariadne. She wore flat leather boots, black jeans and a black top, which was topped off by a black balaclava and shades. He couldn't see her face. In fact, he couldn't see any skin at all as she picked the knife up in a gloved hand before pointing a suppressed gun at the man on the floor. She didn't fire though, she just held him at gunpoint, and the man cowered away from her.

"Ariadne, I might have known you'd show up," Jon said, looking up at her.

She smiled at him as she crouched, the slit on her dress parting as she dropped down, revealing more leg. "Seriously, Jon," she said, her voice sarcastic, "there's no need to thank me, it was my pleasure to save you, really."

Jon grimaced. He didn't like this situation at all. "Thank you," he muttered.

"See, that wasn't so hard, was it?"

"What are you doing here?" he asked, honestly curious.

"Saving your cute ass, I thought that would be obvious."

"But, how?" Had his mind not been spinning from the fight, he could probably have worked it out for himself, but frankly, he was a mess.

"It's simple, Jon. I saw that man threaten you the other day, so I guessed it would only be a matter of time before he showed up again. He knew your name and where you lived, so I knew this was no idle threat. This man had done his homework, and you don't do that if you aren't serious. Good thing I took the threat seriously, don't you think?"

"I guess. Who's your friend?"

"This?" Ariadne asked, waving at the woman in black. "You can call her Solitaire. She's just hired help. Someone who knows their way around a gun, that's all. No one you should concern yourself with. She was just doing what needed to be done." Ariadne looked over at Solitaire and nodded. Solitaire nodded back and approached the man on the floor.

"Get up," she said.

Jon's attacker spat back at her. So Solitaire hit him across the face with her gun. The man grunted and spat blood to the floor. She put the gun to his head.

"Get up, and limp out, or we carry you out."

The man gritted his bloody teeth in barely restrained fury. "Fine," he said, and struggled to his feet while Solitaire watched dispassionately. As he got to his feet, Ariadne stood and walked over to him, her head held high and imperious as she grabbed him by the jaw. Her nails dug into his cheeks.

"We're watching you, David Letov. You and Vassili's other contacts. Jon is not to be harmed, and if I see you or your friends within a hundred metres of him ever again, you will not live to see the next day. Got it? Oh, and say hi to your nephew, Pavel, for me."

David's eyes bugged as Ariadne revealed what she knew about him. As she let go, the man shivered, clearly scared. Solitaire jabbed her gun into his back and followed him as he hopped out of the room and then the house.

Moments later, Jon made out the sound of a sliding van door slamming shut not too far away.

"I'm so sorry you had to see that, Jon," she said with a sigh. "This life can be a messy business, sometimes. But, you know that, don't you."

"Yeah, I do. Thanks, by the way," Jon said again, honestly grateful for her intervention.

She put her hand to her chest, over the cleavage that the fitted dress was doing its best to keep in place. "My, my, actual, honest to goodness gratitude. This is a momentous day, Jon. I'm flattered."

"You did just save my life," Jon said with a shrug.

Ariadne grinned and crouched down again, offering her hand. He took it, and she gripped his arm with her other hand as he got to his feet. "I did save you, didn't I," she said with a smile, that went from warm to icy cold suddenly. "Which means you owe me, Jon. You owe me your life. Remember that."

Jon blinked as a horrible sinking feeling opened up deep inside him as her words sunk in. Oh crap. But as that realisation grew, he considered the situation. Had she set him up, somehow? Was all this a ruse? Was that man honestly from Vassili, or was he sent here by her? Or maybe she'd just taken advantage of the situation and turned it to her favour? Whatever the case, she'd played him masterfully, and he'd walked smiling into her trap, just as he'd known he would.

Ariadne's smile was suddenly full of warmth again. She leaned in and kissed him on the cheek before he could do much to resist. Pulling back, she winked. "Now, I really must fly. I have work to attend to. I'll see you around, Jon," she said and swanned out of his house, shutting the front door behind her.

Jon just stared out from the front room into the hallway, where she'd gone, and then looked down at the patch of blood that had pooled on the old carpet, possibly staining it for good.

With a sigh, Jon collapsed onto his sofa and let out a long, weary sigh as he shook his head in disbelief. He'd been played, he was certain of it. And now he owed her a debt that he might struggle to ever pay off.

Yeah, it was definitely a pizza night.

In fact, it was probably a pizza, chips and beer night. He pulled out his phone.

26

Driving to Kate's and then the hospital the next morning after a fitful night's sleep, Jon did his best to keep his eyes open. If it hadn't been for the frankly crazy thoughts that were spinning around his head, he felt sure he'd have fallen asleep at the wheel.

After being attacked and ordering his pizza, he'd spent the rest of the night stewing over whether he should tell Kate about what had happened. The whole thing seemed absolutely crazy and almost didn't seem real. It was too weird to be real, and yet, the dark red stain on his carpet said otherwise.

A man had been shot in his front room, leaving him with a smashed window—that he'd boarded up—and a ruined carpet.

Well, he'd thought about having the carpet replaced anyway, so this just gave him another reason to get on and do it.

As far as he saw it, he had several options. Tell Kate nothing and hide what had happened, tell her he'd been attacked but had fought the man off himself, or tell her everything, including everything about Ariadne as well.

Hiding it would probably be more way more hassle than it was worth, and might even be impossible. After eating, Jon had attempted to clean up the blood after looking up the best method for getting it out of carpet. He'd made a good go of it, and while the worst of it was gone, the stain was still visible, and he felt sure Kate would notice.

The window was harder to deal with, and for now, he'd settled for hammering a wooden board into place. He'd get that replaced soon enough, but Kate was sure to come over at some point before he'd fixed everything up.

Besides, he hated lying to her, and that was no way to build a relationship. But telling her the truth about Ariadne carried its own issues. For one, he wasn't sure how Ariadne would feel if he was to tell Kate everything. Ariadne was not someone to be trifled with, and she might take exception to him telling people about her. Ariadne might do something to hurt him, or worse still, she might hurt Kate.

The previous night's antics were both harrowing and suspicious, and to Jon's mind, just a little too neat to be pure coincidence. But how much had Ariadne planned? Had she set up the whole thing, or had she just taken advantage of the situation that had been presented to her? Because, if she had set it all up, and had planned for this man to attack him, what was to stop her from getting someone to attack Kate? He certainly wouldn't put it past her to hurt someone who knew more than she was comfortable with, and if Jon caused Kate to get hurt or worse, he wasn't sure he could live with himself. He'd already lost one partner to the actions of a crazed killer. He couldn't lose Kate too.

He couldn't put himself through that.

And so he'd settled on the only choice he felt he could make, and chose to go the middle route.

"Mornin', you dirty stop out," Jon said as he picked Kate up from her flat, on the way to East Surrey Hospital, just south of Redhill. "How you feeling?"

"Good morning, and I'm fine, thank you," she said, leaning over and kissing him briefly. "I didn't go crazy, and we were eating anyway, so..."

"Fair enough," Jon replied with a smile, pleased that she'd been enjoying herself. "You had fun then?"

"Yeah. It's always good to catch up with Harper. We get on so well. I'll have to introduce you sometime. I've told her all about you."

"Oooh, not everything, I hope," he said.

"Of course not. I wouldn't want to scare her off with tales of gravy on chips or deep-fried Mars Bars."

"I think you'll find that's Scotland."

"Whatever, it's all north of the Watford Gap," Kate said with a smile. Jon laughed and met her gaze briefly. She was so full of life with her big green eyes twinkling in the morning light. He knew he'd come to the right choice. There was no way he could ever put her in danger. He just couldn't do it.

She did not need to know about Ariadne. It was just too risky, as far as he was concerned. Was he lying to her? Only by omission, maybe, but this was to protect her, besides, he could always re-evaluate things later. But for now, this was the best course of action. He was sure of it.

"What about you? Did you do much?"

Jon sighed. "Actually, yeah, I had a bit of an eventful night." He met her gaze again, and she must have seen something behind his eyes. The jovial attitude she'd been in just a moment before fell away in an instant to be replaced by a look of concern.

"What happened?" she asked before a look of sudden realisation flashed over her features. "Oh, it wasn't that man, was it?"

Jon nodded. "He attacked me."

"What?!" Kate sounded shocked. "Are you okay? What happened?"

"He jumped me on my doorstep, and we fought for a bit. He pulled a knife."

Kate gasped.

"But I got it off him and cut his leg. He ran off, but not before putting a rock through my window."

"Jesus, are you okay?"

"I'm fine. I was a little shaken, but... I'm okay."

"What did Nathan think?"

Jon blinked at the reply. "I've not told him," Jon said, feeling sure he knew where she was going with this.

"What? Why? You did call it in, right?"

Jon shook his head. "Um, no. I didn't."

"Jon! You have to. You have to log this. You can't let this go. You were attacked by a man with a knife. Are you crazy?"

"It's fine. I'm okay, I'm not hurt, and I don't think it will happen again."

"What? Why? How can you say that?"

"I just have a feeling. The guy seemed pretty scared."

Kate sighed and slumped back into her seat. "You can't do this, Jon. You need to tell someone. I can't have you acting like this. It's madness."

"Okay, okay," Jon replied, suddenly feeling stupid for not calling the police, or at least Nathan. "No, you're right. I should have told someone, but I'd like to keep this internal. Just within the SIU, okay? I don't think I'll be attacked again, so."

"Ugh!" Kate shook her head. "You can be so stupid sometimes, you know that? I just... aagh, men. It's not big or clever to do this, you know. You're not helping yourself. You're just going to make me worry."

Jon realised that she was probably right. He needed to do more than just keep it to himself, even if he did leave out the Ariadne stuff.

"I'm sorry. You're right. I'll tell Nathan, okay?"

"Good. Do it today, please, or I will."

"I'll do it, I promise."

"So, what happened? Who was he?"

"I... I don't know. I've got no idea." That wasn't strictly true of course. He'd heard Ariadne call him David, but who was to say that was actually his name? "He didn't exactly give me his life story."

"Shite. And there's nothing else? He didn't say why he was there?"

"Sorry, no," Jon said, fully aware of how much he was lying. He *thought* he knew why he was there, but he wasn't sure how much he believed it. These facts came from the man himself, and he could just as easily have been lying for all Jon knew. Besides, if he mentioned that the man had been sent from Vassili, Kate would only worry, and he didn't want that.

He needed to protect her and Nathan and the others.

The thing was, he wasn't lying when he said he had a feeling that Vassili wouldn't send any other would-be assassins to kill him. Ariadne was watching, and in the depths of this murky ocean, he got the feeling that Ariadne was a pretty big shark, much bigger than Vassili and ready to eat him alive.

No, he felt sure Vassili would not try this again, he was sure of it, but he couldn't tell Kate that. The best thing was just to downplay it, he thought.

"Jesus, Jon, you're going to give me a heart attack one of these days."

"I know, I'm sorry."

"It's okay. I just worry for you when you tell me things like this."

Jon shrugged and gave her a smile. "I'll try to lead a less eventful life from now on. I'll put a sign on the front door, 'No assassins or hired goons', okay? That should do the trick."

She smirked. "Good, you do that."

The trip to the hospital didn't take that long. They were soon parked up and making their way inside, when Jon spotted someone walking out that he recognised.

"Mr Woods?" Jon called out.

Lenny stopped and looked over, he looked shocked. "Oh, detectives."

Jon eyed the bandages on his nose and the black eyes that he sported.

"Are you okay, Mr Woods?"

"You look like you've been in a fight," Kate said.

"No, no. Nothing like that," Lenny replied. "I just… fell, you know? I tripped up and smashed my face into something. It's silly, my own fault really."

"Are you sure you're okay? That looks pretty nasty," Kate said."

"Yeah, I'm fine."

"How's your daughter?" Kate asked.

"She's fine. She's with her Nana."

"And your wife?" Jon said.

"Oh, um, I think she's with them."

"You think…?

"No, she is. She had to pop out for something. Then I was trying to look after Gracie and things got a little hectic and, I fell."

"I see. Well, I hope you're okay."

"I'm fine. How's the case coming along?"

"We're following up on some leads, I think we're close to finding the killer."

"Oh good, that's great news. Thank you."

"My pleasure," Jon replied. He seemed massively distracted, like he just wanted to get away. Jon wasn't sure why, and as for him falling… Well, Jon had seen broken noses before, and he had a feeling that Mr Woods was not being totally honest here. As for why, he couldn't say, but they didn't have the time right now, and if Lenny wasn't going to be honest, then there was little they could do. Letting him go, they made their way inside and soon found the Ward they were looking for.

Introducing themselves to the duty nurse, she kindly informed them that Helen had responded well to their treatments and could probably talk to them.

Within moments they were walking into the ward where Jon spotted Mark sitting with his sister. She was looking much better than when he'd seen her being pulled from the wall.

"Detectives," Mark said in greeting as they walked over.

"Hello, Mark," Kate said.

"Good morning," Jon said to them both.

"Is this is a bad time?" the nurse asked. "You don't have to talk yet."

"No, I want to, thank you," Helen replied.

"Okay, well, call me in if you need me, okay?" the nurse said, before leaving them.

Helen smiled up at them. "Are you the ones who found me?"

"Kind of," Jon answered. "I'm DCI Jon Pilgrim, and this is DS Kate O'Connell. I'm pleased to see you alive and well."

"Thanks, me too," Helen smiled.

"And me," Mark added.

"How did you know where I was?"

"We didn't. But we did find your purse in the basement, hidden behind some other things in there. And when we were interviewing Mark, he called you on your private phone, which happened to be discarded in the concealed partition. The officers doing a forensics sweep of the basement heard it ring, and that led us to you."

"Aaah, okay. That was lucky."

"I know. So I suppose the person you have to thank the most is your brother. If he hadn't called you, we might never have found you."

Helen smiled and looked up at Mark, taking his hand in hers. "Thank you."

Mark shrugged. "I couldn't not call you," he said, before they hugged.

"Can we ask you a few questions?" Jon asked, as Mark pulled away.

"Of course," she replied.

"I'll get out of your hair," Mark said, moving away from the bed.

"You don't need to go," Helen said.

"It's fine. I need a drink anyway. I'll be back when they're done, okay?" Mark said and left with a smile.

"How are you feeling?" Kate asked her.

"I'm okay. As good as can be expected, I suppose. The doctors say I should make a full recovery."

"That's great news," Kate said, as Jon noticed the bruising and the bandages on her wrists. She had a way to go yet.

"I saw him," she said.

"What? Do you mean the person who did this to you?" Jon asked.

"Yes. I saw his face. I know what he looks like. I'd recognise him. I know it."

"You're sure?" Kate asked.

"Positive."

"Okay." Kate glanced up at Jon. He nodded to her, knowing what she was thinking, and as he watched, Kate pulled out several photos of the main suspects on the case and placed them before her. "These are the main suspects. Do you recognise anyone?"

She nodded and pointed to the photo on the right. "It was him."

"Are you sure?"

"One-hundred-percent. I'll never forget that face, it will haunt my nightmares. It was him."

"You have to be totally sure," Jon said.

"I am, completely. It was him. What's his name?"

"I'd rather not say right this moment," Jon replied. "You'll find out in due course, though."

"Okay, thank you," Kate said, and picked up the photos.

"Why were you there?" Jon asked.

"I was looking for Mark. He'd rented that house just weeks before, and I'd seen him there. But he was getting all obsessed with Duncan again, and it just wasn't healthy, so I went to see if I could talk him out of it."

"But, Mark wasn't in?"

"No. But the front door was open, and so was the basement door, so I went to have a look. There was no one there, though, so I turned out the light to head back upstairs. That's when he jumped me. I was in and out of consciousness until I suddenly woke up in that wall, with those other bodies."

Kate reached out and took Helen's hand in hers to help comfort her. "It's okay. You're safe now."

"I know, thank you."

"We'll be talking to you much more over the next few days," Jon said.

"That's okay. Anything I can do to help. Anything."

"Okay, rest up," Jon said, as he heard a raised voice from the corridor outside. Turning to look, he saw Mark had returned with a coffee and was standing facing his parents, Robert and Rose. They did not look happy.

Saying a quick goodbye, Jon strode from the ward, out into the corridor and reception area.

"She doesn't need you here," Robert said to his son, venom in his words.

"She needs me more than you and your hate," Mark snapped back.

"Hey," Jon said, putting as much authority into his voice as he could. Nurses were heading over, but he waved them back as he lowered his voice without losing any of the steel he'd put into it. "Be quiet. No one in here wants to hear you arguing. If you want to shout and scream, go outside. But I can tell you that Helen does not want to hear it. She has been through a literal nightmare and came within touching distance of death. What she needs right now is all the love and support you can give. She does not need any fighting or squabbling, and neither does anyone else in here. So grow up and put your differences to one side for once. And if you can't do that, I'll drag you outside myself. Understand?"

They all nodded, looking sullen as if they were kids again being told off by their teacher.

"Good, now I've got a killer to catch, so if you don't mind, I'd like to get on with that. Is that okay?"

27

The drive across the county seemed to take three times as long as it usually did, but Jon knew that this was all in his head. It was an illusion brought on by his need to get to the killer as quickly as possible and make sure that he never did any of this again.

They needed to find him and stop him before he killed again. He had to admit to being a little surprised by Helen's statement and who she said had sealed her up in the wall, but she'd been certain, and he was not in the business of second-guessing someone who'd stared death in the face and come away alive. Helen said she recognised him, and Jon believed her.

As he drove over there, he wondered what they would find.

Would he know they were coming for him? Would he be prepared for them, and how would he react? He had to be prepared for violence, which was part of the reason why they had coordinated with base to meet up with several marked cars and officers to do this properly.

He didn't fancy storming into this one half-cocked and run the risk of getting either himself or Kate hurt in the process. Plus, there was the issue of the complaints he'd had over the last few days, and making sure there was nothing else that might rear its head and ruin the case for them.

Stingray would be most unimpressed with any heroics.

As they got close, they met up with the other officers and made their way over in convoy, complete with a warrant to search his house.

Eventually, they pulled up outside the house and walked the short distance up to the front door and knocked. Jon felt the familiar feel of adrenaline rush through his system, filling him with energy as he waited for the confrontation with this killer.

Moments later, the door opened and a man appeared.

"Duncan Reid," Jon said, noting how he was wearing only his underwear. "Would you mind just stepping outside for a moment?"

"Um, of course, what is this about?" he asked as he stepped out from the house. As he moved, Jon picked up a distinct whiff of something coming from inside. It was a smell he knew well. The smell of death.

"I am arresting you on Suspicion of Murder—"

"No. No, it's not me," Duncan pleaded, his voice weak.

Jon frowned.

"Duncan?" The voice came from inside. Jon turned and watched in mute horror as Mrs Woods, came swanning around the corner into the hall wearing some black, lacy lingerie and heels. "What are you doing?"

She was picking something from her nails, and only looked up after a few steps.

Phoebe Woods froze as her eyes met Jon's and a look of horror appeared on her face.

"It was her," Duncan cried out. "She did it. She made me help her."

For a moment, all Jon could do was stare at her as he tried to process what the hell was going on. A second later, tottering on precarious heels, she turned and fled from the corridor. Kate raced past him into the house.

Seeing her run by, Jon got a hold of himself and ran in after Kate. He rushed into the room on the right where Phoebe had disappeared. The floor was covered in a plastic sheet with smears of blood on it. In the middle of the sheet was a human shape, wrapped in black plastic.

Another victim.

Kate dashed across the room and through a door towards the rear of the house. Jon followed, and appeared in the kitchen behind Kate who'd stopped just on the other side of the door. Phoebe stood facing them, a large kitchen knife in her hands, her eyes wild.

"Don't come any closer."

"It's over, Phoebe," Jon said. He could still hear Duncan at the front of the house, shouting, saying she was the killer.

"No, it's not over. It's never over."

"Put the knife down," Kate said.

"I didn't do it," Phoebe stammered, as two more uniformed officers entered the kitchen from another door. Phoebe sniffed and dropped the knife before she leant against the counter and let out a sob. "I didn't make him do anything, it was him. It was Duncan, he made me. You have to believe me."

Something seemed to fall into place in his mind as she spoke, and Jon started to feel like he was making sense of it. "You broke your husband's nose, didn't you."

"What?"

"I bet when he finds out where we found you, I think he might admit that it was you who hurt him, right?"

Phoebe locked eyes with Jon, all emotion gone as Kate stepped closer and kicked the knife away.

"I'm right, aren't I?" Jon asked as Kate moved behind Phoebe and cuffed her.

Phoebe said nothing, but her demeanour had changed. The act of being the victim was gone, replaced by something strong, defiant, and devoid of emotion.

"Get some clothes on her," Jon said, as Kate guided Phoebe out of the kitchen, aided by a female uniformed officer who'd just walked in to help.

As they took her off, Jon walked back outside to find Duncan cuffed, but still ranting.

"It was her, she killed them. She did it. I didn't kill anyone."

"Mr Reid," Jon said, stepping closer. "So, if you didn't kill anyone, why would Helen Cooper say you were the one who sealed her up in the wall?"

Duncan sighed. "Yeah, I did that. But I didn't kill her."

"You nearly did."

"She interrupted me, I had to do something. I panicked."

"And the body inside, in the plastic bags?"

Duncan suddenly sobbed and fell to his knees. It looked like his strength had suddenly left him, as he cried out. Jon watched in confusion and surprise as Duncan's emotions took over. After a moment, Jon crouched down before him.

"Who was it?"

"Corey," Duncan muttered between desperate sniffs. "It was Corey."

"Corey Grant?" Jon asked, wanting to be sure they were talking about the same man.

"Yes," Duncan confirmed. "It was her idea. She made me contact him. She made me bring him here."

221

"And she killed him?"

Duncan nodded. "She made me help her. She just gets in my head, and I have to do what she wants."

"I understand," Jon said, standing back up while a Uniform brought Duncan back to his feet. Turning, Jon saw Kate walk Phoebe back out of the house, fully dressed again, her expression stony, and the look in her eyes was as terrifying as it was hollow.

"I'm sorry, Phoebe. I'm so sorry. Please, you'll forgive me, won't you? I want to see you again."

But Phoebe didn't look at him or even seem to register that he was there at all. She just walked with the officers that were accompanying her, getting into the back of one of the cars.

Jon turned to another officer. "Take him too," he said, and watched as Duncan was led away.

"So, it was Phoebe?" Kate asked as she walked over to Jon.

"My gut says it's her, but Duncan's involved. For sure. I just don't know by how much."

"And, do we know who's in the bag, inside?"

"Duncan says it's Corey Grant, his former tenant."

"Shite," Kate said. "Looks like we have our work cut out for us unravelling this one."

"Yeah," Jon agreed, as he looked back at Duncan's house.

28

"Well, at least you got your woman in the end," Detective Superintendent Ray Johnston said, sitting on the opposite side of the desk.

"Thank you. We think so, yes."

"And yet, we had her here, on literally the first day of the case. You interviewed her downstairs."

Jon nodded, feeling sheepish. "We did, yes."

"We had her, and we let her go."

"There was no reason to suspect her at the time," Jon replied, feeling confident anyone else would have done the exact same thing.

"Perhaps, but you can imagine how this looks on the surface to the likes of the ACC and others."

"I understand."

"Do you?" Ray snapped.

"Sir, we saved a young girl from a grim fate, and we found the killer."

"I know that Jon, but it doesn't make it look any better. As far as the powers that be will care, it really doesn't matter."

Jon nodded.

Ray sighed. "Look, I know you've done a good job. You did only what anyone else would have done, but you need to do

223

better than this. For what it's worth though, I think you should be proud of your team for their work on this case.

"Thank you, sir."

Ray held his gaze for a moment and took a breath. "I know why you think I'm here, Jon. I know what you think of me. I'm not stupid, and neither are you. To a degree, you're right, the ACC did send me here, and he did ask certain things of me. But I'm not here to discredit you or destroy this unit from within. I've got to where I am by playing by the rules. I strive for excellence every day, and I expect all those under my command to do the same. However, by far the most important thing is that we protect lives and serve the public. That is priority number one for me, and always will be."

"Mine too."

"Good. But I know you can be a little reckless sometimes, Jon, and I'm here to make sure you follow the rules. I expect results, and I expect excellence. Your behaviour on this case was a little, um... on the edge of acceptable, and it was noticed. I think you need to be a little more careful. You and Kate, but mostly you. While I'm not here to find fault and shut the unit down, if you're *not* careful, you will do that on your own without any help from me. Do you understand?"

"I think so, sir," Jon replied, feeling somewhat surprised by Stingray's little speech.

"You've stepped on some toes, Jon, and these people do not forget about this kind of thing. They take it personally and will be on the lookout for ways to stomp on your feet with steel-toe-capped boots. So I would suggest you don't give them the chance."

"I'll do my best, sir."

"I hope so. I really do. Good work, now go and do your job."

"Will do, sir," Jon said and left the office behind.

Walking back into the SIU office, Jon spotted Kate talking to Nathan and walked over.

"How'd that go?" Kate asked.

"As well as can be expected," Jon replied. "It felt like both a pat on the back and a rap across the knuckles."

"Well, you're still here, the SIU's still here, and another killer is in custody. I'd call that a win," Kate declared.

"Me too," Nathan agreed.

Jon smiled. "I guess I should always look on the bright side."

"You should," Kate replied.

"Okay, so anything new for me?"

"Actually, yes," Nathan said. "This has been all across the news by now, of course. And because of that and also because of our questioning of the Miller boys, we've had a walk-in."

"Go on," Jon replied.

"Well, he agreed to talk on condition of anonymity, which I agreed to. He's a Miller, and he's also a former lover of Corey Grant."

"Okay," Jon said. "So, what did he say?"

"He said that Corey had always struggled with his sexuality. Has done for years. He said Corey had a fling with Duncan that was on and off his entire tenancy of the house in Newdigate. It seems that Corey didn't want the Miller family knowing that he liked men, as he didn't think they'd approve. He thought it might make some of the guys nervous, or not want to work with him, and he needed the work and the money."

"I see."

"So anyway, this guy got in touch with Corey about a week ago. They met up and had a drink, but that was the last he saw of Corey. Apparently, Duncan had been in touch and wanted to see Corey. That was the last this walk-in saw of Corey."

"Because Duncan killed him," Jon said.

"Yep."

"Okay, thank you, Nathan."

"Jon," Kate said, giving him a look. "Did you have something else to tell Nathan about?"

"Huh?" Jon said before the penny dropped, and he realised what she was talking about. "Oh, yeah. Have you got a moment, in my office, Nathan?"

"Um, yeah, sure guv," Nathan replied, before Jon turned and led Nathan across the room and into his office at the far side. He shut the door and sat behind his desk.

"What's up?" Nathan asked.

"I've been keeping this to myself... well, Kate and myself, but she thinks I need to tell more people, like you."

"I'm all ears."

"I was attacked at my home last night." Jon launched into the same story he'd told Kate, being careful to leave anything about Ariadne out.

"I see," Nathan replied as Jon finished the tale.

"I know I should have reported it, but I don't want to make a fuss, and I honestly think I've dealt with it. But Kate wanted me to tell you, okay?"

"Well, I'm not sure you've really dealt with anything, and it's not good that someone out there knows where you live."

Jon shrugged. "Fair point."

"I've got some connections at High Down Prison. Want me to see what they can find out?"

Jon nodded. "Okay, yeah, sure. Thanks."

"No problem, and... be careful, Jon."

29

Jon sat at the table beside Kate, and looked up into the stone-cold eyes of Phoebe Woods. She stared at him, and for Jon, it felt like he was staring into a deep, dark pit. The eyes were often called a window to the soul. They were often the place where some kind of truth lay, where you could get a feel for a person. They would often betray someone's true motives or thoughts, giving people like Jon an insight into the person they were talking to.

But with Phoebe, Jon didn't get that feeling at all. There was almost something missing there, and as he stared into the woman's eyes, it was almost as if this woman didn't have a soul.

Her eyes were empty, and emotionless as she sat opposite, staring at them, her solicitor beside her.

"We've spoken with both Duncan and your husband, Lenny, Mrs Woods."

"Good," she replied.

"Mr Woods was most surprised to hear where we found you. He was most upset, and he admitted that it was you who attacked him."

Phoebe shrugged.

"You wanted to go out, didn't you? You were living in a hotel room while all this was going on. He said you were agitated, that you had been for days. He said you were bad tempered and that you insisted on going out, but he wasn't happy with you doing this and you argued. You don't argue over much according to him but he felt that you shouldn't be going out for hours on end while this was going on, and he put his foot down. But you didn't like that, did you, Mrs Woods? You got upset and you broke your husband's nose, before going out anyway."

Again, Phoebe said nothing, she just stared back at Jon, listening, but showing no emotion or reaction at all.

"But, it's not the first time you've displayed questionable behaviour, is it? You first met as teenagers, right? Mr Woods said you've always been a little obsessive, even back then. He said that you seemed to decide that he was going to be your man, and that was that. He said you dated for a while, but he broke it off as he wanted to see other people, only for you to stalk him, follow him, confront his friends and girlfriends until you eventually won him back."

Again, Phoebe said nothing. It was as if she was a statue as she sat, unmoving, just listening. The whole act was incredibly unnerving.

"I was wondering where all this came from," Jon said. "So, we looked into your family and asked Mr Woods what he

229

knew too, and what we know is that you were the middle of three girls born to your parents. Your younger sister died of meningitis while you were young, and that led to your parents fighting until they broke up and your father left you all. Then your mother was violent towards you both, according to your sister who we've had a nice chat with. But she ran away, didn't she, leaving you with your violent mother."

"Care to elaborate on that point?" Kate asked, but she was greeted with silence.

"Okay, well, let's extrapolate, shall we?" Jon said. "I'm guessing that at some point you killed someone. Maybe you didn't mean to, maybe you did. But you liked it, and for whatever reason, you got away with it. But the high you got from that kill didn't last, and you had to do it again. But you needed to be smart. You needed to be careful. You couldn't rely on luck. I don't know if this was before or after you met Lenny, but if I had to guess, I'd say before. Certainly, before you married, anyway. How am I doing, so far?"

Phoebe chewed on her lip, but said nothing.

"Phoebe," Kate said. "There are people out there with missing sons and daughters. We've been able to give peace to some of them, the ones we've found, but I'm guessing there's more. With the testimony of your husband and Duncan, I think it's highly likely you'll see life for this, no matter what.

So, why hold out? Help us, and maybe we can give these people some peace."

Phoebe sighed. "The first one was before I met Lenny," she said. "You're right, it was on a whim. It was easy. Too easy, and it made me feel good. I burnt him, and no one came. No police came to my door. No national manhunt. Nothing. So, I wanted to do it again. I met Lenny later. I needed a husband. I needed to look... normal, I guess."

"You're saying you're not normal?"

"I'm saying that I recognise that I am not like other people. I don't feel things in the same way, and most people don't kill people. So, I needed to look normal. A husband and a family would help me do that. Lenny was perfect."

"Were you still killing?"

"Not in the home." Phoebe smiled, but didn't elaborate.

"Duncan said you two met on a night out. One of your hunts for a victim, was it?"

"I was out drinking," Phoebe said.

"This was after you were married?"

"Of course," she replied. "Lenny does as I ask, he knows better than to say no. It was about two years after we were married. A year after Gracie was born."

"I see," Jon replied. He remembered the daughter and felt shocked by how casually she inserted her daughter into the conversation about how she'd been killing countless people.

231

He was also getting a clearer understanding the nature of her relationship with Lenny, and who was in charge. There was no mutual partnership here. Phoebe was in control of everything. Lenny had explained how she controlled the money, how his wages got paid into her account, and she handed out money as she saw fit, how she controlled which friends he could see and when. She'd control and confiscate his phone, and often reply as him. She controlled everything, and he just went along with it.

"Duncan said you tried to kill him, is that right?"

"He fought me off," Phoebe replied. "But he wasn't upset. We'd been seeing each other for a few weeks before the opportunity presented itself, but I underestimated him. But he was curious. He wanted to know if I'd done it before. He wanted to help."

"I get the impression that he's a little obsessed with you," Kate said.

"He had his uses," Phoebe replied.

"Such as for hiding bodies?"

"He helped me dispose of them," she admitted. "He saw the hollow centre in the wall of his mother's house when he let Corey do some renovation work, and thought it would make a good hiding place."

"What about for finding victims?" Jon asked. "He helped with that too, right?"

"I think you know well enough that he did. I'm guessing he told you that he would help look for people. The lonely, the dispossessed, people who would not be missed. We both got quite good at finding them. Corey was supposed to be one, but Duncan resisted."

"And then there was Mark."

"I think so?"

"He was. Duncan explained how he seduced him, but he changed his mind when Mark's sister called while Duncan was with him. He'd be missed, and people would come looking, so he decided not to bring him to you. That of course led to a long term relationship, though, which it seems like Duncan struggled with."

Phoebe shrugged. "I don't give a shit about that."

"So, let's get back to these houses," Jon said. "Duncan inherited his mother's house when she died, rented it out to earn money while he helped you. When Corey did some work, he revealed the hollow wall, which led to Duncan dumping bodies in there while Corey was on holiday. Later, Corey left after Duncan had an argument, and he then rented a place from Polly for you to use as a dumping ground. It was good because it had a basement that Polly didn't like to go into. So, Duncan built a partition with a hidden door and you used that, until someone interrupted him."

Phoebe rolled her eyes. "Idiot."

"You didn't plan on that happening, did you. Mark's sister went looking for Mark, and stumbled on Duncan working in the basement. He panicked and attacked her, but he couldn't kill her, because while he might help you, he's never actually killed anyone, has he?"

"He's weak, like you all are," Phoebe replied.

"So he sealed her up in the wall, but he was rushing. He wasn't careful and left clues behind which led to us finding Miss Cooper, and her leading us to Duncan, and you. But you weren't happy, were you? Is that why you forced Duncan to call Corey? Was it punishment for him to see his friend be killed by you?"

She didn't answer.

"One thing I don't understand," Kate said, leaning forward. "Why move into the house where Duncan was hiding bodies? You knew the bodies were in the walls, so why move in there? Isn't that a little risky?"

Phoebe smiled. "That's why I did it. I wanted to be close to them. I wanted to take that risk. I was curious to see what I could get away with."

"Is that why you let your husband start renovations?" Jon asked. "You knew what he'd find in that wall."

"I did. I was curious. I wanted to see them, and I was going to try to pin it on someone. Duncan or Evan maybe."

"But Duncan messed up, and attacked Helen," Jon said.

Phoebe's smile faded. "Like I said, idiot."

Jon nodded, and knew he had his work cut out for him. They had a lot to go through here, and they could only hope that she would admit to the other murders and tell them who she'd killed.

"Alright, let's start from the beginning again," Jon said.

30

"Thanks for coming over to see us, Ellie," Jon said as he stood up and gestured to the room around him. "What do you think? Is it everything you hoped for?"

"It's pretty nice, I have to say," she answered. "And, thanks for having me."

"No problem," Kate said. "Come over any time you like."

"I will."

"Send my regards to DI Taylor, won't you?"

"Oh, of course. I'll be sure to. He's been in a bad mood ever since you turned up at the house in Redhill."

"I always knew he was a mardy bugger," Jon said.

"A what?" Kate asked. "What's a *mardy* bugger?"

"A grumpy git," Jon explained. "Do you not know what mardy means?"

"Obviously not." Kate turned to Ellie. "Sorry, he's northern."

"Northern?" Ellie asked, smiling, dropping her voice into a stage whisper. "How'd he get down here then? How'd he get past the fences?"

"I don't know. Work visa, maybe?" Kate suggested.

"He filled out a form?" Ellie said, shocked. "I didn't think they knew how to write."

"Yeah, yeah, very funny, girls. Laugh it up."

"Every now and then," Kate continued, her voice taking on a reverential tone, "I think there's a genetic mutation, and a northerner is born with close to average intelligence. I think he's one of these mystical beasts."

"Are you saying… he's the chosen one?"

"The one northerner, chosen to represent his tribe and serve the capital."

"This is some Hunger Games shit," Jon said with a raised eyebrow, and the two women laughed. "Right, I'm popping home for a bit. I'll be round yours later, okay?" he said to Kate.

"Yeah, sure. I'll see you then," Kate said with a smile and a wink.

"Good to see you, Ellie. Don't let DI Taylor cause you too many problems."

"I won't. See ya."

Jon waved and walked out, listening to the two of them laugh again as he left the office behind. He was just glad to be out of there and away from the circus, finally. The interviews with Phoebe had been going on for ages, it seemed. There was so much to go through, and she was admitting to murders they had no idea about.

But Jon had frankly had enough for the day and was glad to be in his car, with the windows down, letting the wind rush through his hair as he drove back home. The week had certainly been one of the more stressful ones he'd experienced in his time, not least of all because of Ariadne, and his stalker.

During a quiet moment, he'd input the name David Letov into the database to see what he could find on him, and sure enough, he was a known associate of Vassili. A low-level thug who'd already served time for violence and similar crimes.

His heart had sunk a little on reading that. He'd hoped that David was a plant, someone who Ariadne had arranged, who didn't have links to Vassili or anyone else. At least that way he was less likely to spread his address around.

But he'd not been quite so lucky, and there was every chance that his address was circulating around the criminal fraternity. That was not a comforting thought.

But there was more to it than just that, because it meant that Ariadne might not have planned it as much as he thought she might have. It meant that to some degree, she'd just taken advantage of the situation and used it to lay a trap for him.

If he had proof that she'd planned it, then he could probably have told her to stuff the favour he apparently owed her up her arse. But it seemed like she'd been telling the truth, and maybe he really did owe her his life.

That, along with the fallout from the case and finding out that Phoebe was a prolific killer, had taken its toll on him today. Now all he wanted to do was to get home, have a shower, and then go and see Kate later. He planned on collapsing on her sofa and falling asleep.

He hoped she wouldn't mind, but he wasn't sure he could keep his eyes open much longer.

As he approached his home, he started to feel the familiar anxiety that maybe Ariadne was there waiting for him again. But it soon became clear that she had taken the night off and wasn't out to torment him tonight, which he felt grateful for, until he turned into the short path up to his house, and he heard a voice behind him.

"DCI Pilgrim, you're home late."

Jon stopped dead in his tracks, feeling angry that this shit should happen again. And as he turned, he spotted a familiar face getting out of a nearby car.

It was Irving Miller. He closed the door behind him and leant against the side of the saloon, his hands in his pockets.

"I'm getting sick of people turning up on my doorstep like this," he said.

"I'm not the first then, I take it," he said and pointed to the boarded-up window.

"No, you're not."

"Well, not that it will make any difference, but I am sorry you've had some unsavoury visitors. Please be assured, they did not come from me."

Jon sighed. "I know. What can I do for you, Mr Miller?"

"Well, firstly, congratulations on the new house, it's a beaut. You've done well for yourself, my son."

Jon raised an eyebrow at the 'son' comment, but let it go. "Thank you," he replied, keen to keep things cordial. "I take it you know what happened to Corey by now?"

"Indeed I do. I'm sorry he passed like that, he was a good guy. He didn't deserve to die, not like that."

"No, he didn't. So, why are you here? Surely it wasn't just to discuss Corey?"

"No, it was not." He cleared his throat. "Are you aware of a man called Terry Sims?"

Jon couldn't help but raise his eyebrows. "The escaped convict?" he asked.

"Indeed, the one your plucky partner arrested with Nathan."

"I'm aware of him, yes."

"Do you know where he might be?"

"Sorry, no," Jon replied, shaking his head. "Do you?"

"Unfortunately not, and that concerns me, Jon. He's already causing ripples within my organisation and within other, similar groups."

"You mean in other gangs?"

"If that is your preferred name for us."

"It's what you are, Irving."

"We're a family, Jon, with a family business."

"Of course you are."

"From what I hear, he's recruiting people. He's already got some of his old gang back with him."

"I see," Jon said. "And do you know what he's planning?"

"No idea, and that's another thing that concerns me."

Jon weighed up what Mr Miller was telling him. He didn't really know this Terry Sims, he'd never met the man, but from what he'd gleaned from Kate, Nathan, and the database, he knew he was not a man to the trifled with. He was an intelligent, violent thug, and everything he knew suggested he was not someone he should underestimate.

"I suggest you keep an eye out, Detective. You never know what's coming around the corner."

"Point taken," Jon replied.

Irving nodded. "Good evening to you, Jon." And with that, he was back into his car and pulling away into the night, leaving Jon alone on his doorstep once more. Looking around, he waited a moment to see if anyone else was about to show up, but there was nothing and no one about.

Figuring he was safe for now, he entered his house and walked back into the kitchen, and stopped short, just inside the doorway. For a moment, he wondered if he'd somehow walked into the wrong house, but a glance back into the hall and the other rooms revealed that he was indeed in the right one.

Jon turned back into the kitchen and admired the brand new oven, washing machine and dishwasher that had been fully installed into his kitchen. They were nice ones too.

"What the hell?" he muttered as his eyes fell onto the bottle of champagne on the table and the note propped up beside it. Without looking, he had a fairly good idea of who'd done this, and after grabbing the note and ripping it open, his suspicions were quickly confirmed.

Jon.

Well done on another successful case. I knew you had it in you.

Enjoy your new kitchen.

Kisses,

Ariadne.

"Well shit," Jon grunted.

As he stared at the note, he noticed another slip of paper by the bottle and picked it up. This one was a newspaper clipping from a side story, telling of the death of David Letrov, the man who attacked him the other night.

242

He'd been found dead, floating in a local river.

"Jesus, Ariadne, was that you? What the hell are you up to?"

THE END

Book 5

A Second Chance

is available for pre-order now.

Click here;

amazon.co.uk/dp/B0985XRHLN/

Author Note

Wow, so here we are at book four of the DCI Pilgrim series, and I couldn't be happier with how it's going.

I'm really pleased with the series so far and the developing relationship between Jon and Kate and the rest of the team. Also, I'm slowly building plans for future books and working out where parts of this are going.

I love writing the Sydney/Ariadne scenes. She's a real cool customer and someone who can challenge Jon in so many ways.

I'm looking forward to diving into book 5, and I have a good idea of what that book will be already.

I hope you enjoyed this book. If you did, please consider leaving a review on Amazon, and I'll see you in book 5.

Also, if you want to interact with me more on Facebook, please consider joining my FB group, here:
www.facebook.com/groups/alfraine.readers

Kindest Regards,
A L Fraine.

www.alfraineauthor.co.uk

Printed in Great Britain
by Amazon

24328721R00138